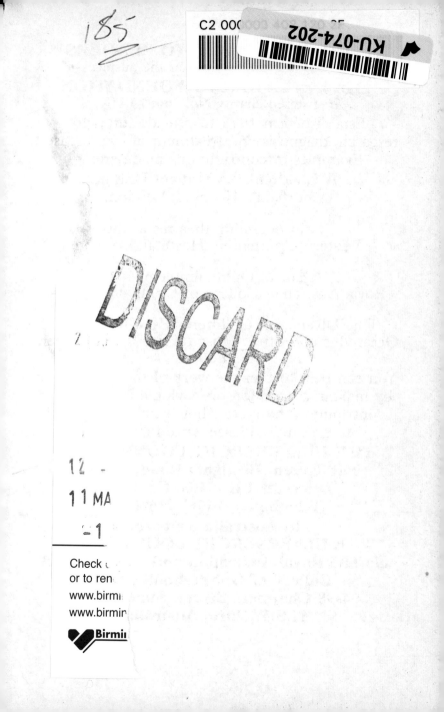

185

KU-074-202

C2 000

THE BALINESE PEARLS

In his screwiest case ever, investigator Harry Ingram becomes enmeshed in beautiful women, dangerous intrigue and double dealing in his search for the missing Balinese Pearls. There is sudden death, too, as Ingram tries to penetrate the hidden motives of a glamorous young heiress and the strange characters who have designs on her money. And in the rapidly moving chain of events in the tropical paradise of Bali, eastern beliefs and tradition clash with the brash materialism of western intruders.

LEE LAMBERT

THE BALINESE PEARLS

Complete and Unabridged

LINFORD
Leicester

First published in Great Britain in 1982 by
Robert Hale Limited
London

First Linford Edition
published 2004
by arrangement with
Robert Hale Limited
London

British Library CIP Data

Lambert, Lee
    The Balinese pearls.—Large print ed.—
Linford mystery library
    1. Detective and mystery stories
    2. Large type books
    I. Title
    823.9'14 [F]

    ISBN 1–84395–321–8

Published by
F. A. Thorpe (Publishing)
Anstey, Leicestershire

Set by Words & Graphics Ltd.
Anstey, Leicestershire
Printed and bound in Great Britain by
T. J. International Ltd., Padstow, Cornwall

This book is printed on acid-free paper

1

Garuda flight GA 642, a Boeing 737 shimmered in the unclouded blueness above the fuming volcanoes of eastern Java and began its slow descent across the strait to Denpasar. The plane turned and came in low over the sea, so low it was inevitable it must touch the racing water beneath. But the sea ended at last in the levelled rubble of the shoreline and tyres screamed on concrete.

A slim, small man in a dapper brown uniform, olive-skinned impassive face, opened my passport and examined the visa indifferently. I hiked my bag into the foyer and found the desk labelled 'Hotel Bali'. It was unmanned. The neighbouring desks for the Bali Beach, Bali Hyatt and Bali Hilton told me collectively to get a taxi. I went out into the sunshine and the steambath heat and did just that. With the windows let all the way down to admit the quietly warm breeze from the sea, the steel box of the ancient Holden was not quite as hot as a blast furnace plant. The driver was a squat, chunky man with a heavy mass of greasy black hair and very white regular teeth when he smiled. He smiled quite a lot as we drifted along the narrow road away from the airport, past the children playing in the drainage ditch, the gaily robed straight-backed women with large bundles on their heads, the white-shirted men on bicycles and roaring Hondas and Suzukis.

'You are the first time in Bali, sir?' the driver asked.

'No, not the first time. Second time. I was here nearly ten years ago.'

He was silent for a minute or two.

'Bali Hotel, sir? Very old hotel. In the town, not near beach.'

'Yes, I know. Oldest hotel on the island. Built by the Dutch when they were here — all of fifty years ago. I like old-fashioned hotels, and I don't like the sort of people you get in the new ones.'

The driver declined to comment. I

had a mind's eye picture of the pool at the Bali International, the water full of screaming kids, the terrace cluttered by paunchy Australians swigging their San Miguel and totally ignoring their bulging women in gaudy bikinis who insisted on exposing what was better not exposed.

'No,' I resumed, 'I like the quiet places. And besides I like Denpasar. I find it interesting.'

The driver smiled again at that and let a mile or two of narrow tarmac and some dozens of bodies and bikes drift by.

'You are travelling on your own, sir? No lady?'

'That's right. No lady.'

He was silent again. I could see him eyeing me in his driving mirror, making up his mind about something.

'You like girl, sir? Nice girl, very young, very pretty — only five thousand rupiah? Very cheap.'

He turned and grinned at me.

'I'm sure she's worth much more,' I grinned back. 'But thank you, no.'

He was silent again for another mile.

'Boy, sir? Nice young boy, sir? What about a boy?'

'No, not my style.'

He pursed his lips. His voice assumed a high, slightly desperate note.

'Temple dancing, sir? You like to see Kechak, Barong, Legong dance? Legong dance very nice, all girls.'

'No, I've seen all that.'

I saw him look at me again, shrug his shoulders and shake his head slightly. We were in the town now and turning down a broad avenue with large, glaringly white buildings on either hand. A few hundred yards and the car swung into a driveway. There was a white porch with entrance doors and a long screen that hid the interior of the hotel from the road.

'Bali Hotel, sir.'

I paid him off and dumped my bag in the entrance hall. 'Sorry we couldn't do business,' I waved back at him. He drove away still smiling.

A tall sober girl at the desk told me about the rooms. I opted for one a little way back from the pool that boasted air-conditioning and its own bathroom. A small bow-legged porter in a coloured sarong and white jacket took my bag and I followed him along the side of the pool and down a path across a strip of closely cropped grass. In the room I stripped off my creased and sticky travel clothes, showered and put on lightweight slacks and a T-shirt. I buttoned a fold of rupiah in the back pocket of the slacks and checked a number in my pocket book. Then I walked back by the pool and over to the lobby and asked for the telephone.

A woman answered my call, her voice low-pitched, not unattractive, but with that certain rasp in it that all American women seem to have.

'Who is that speaking?' I asked. The voice told me its name and I repeated it across the crackle of the line. 'Jacky? Jacky Marczak? Yes, I have it now. Miss Marczak, I would like to speak to Miss Valence. Ingram is the name.' I was asked to wait a moment.

Clicks from the phone as it was put down at the other end and a pause. Then more clicks and another woman's voice came across the line, an American voice too, but softer and still deeper and immediately disproving my theory of the universal rasp.

'This is Andrée Valence speaking.'

'I believe you are expecting my call, Miss Valence,' I said. 'Ingram, Harry Ingram. I think you know what it's about. I want to come out and see you . . . Yes, as soon as possible, please. I have to see you about the pearls. The Balinese pearls.'

2

Twenty minutes later I was in another cab going north out of Denpasar and then heading east, climbing all the time, through little places like Tjeluk, Batuan, Mas and Ubud, places where they make the filigree silver and weave the hand-made batiks and paint the green and blue people-crowded paintings that dazzle the eye. There was a succession of large bungalows separated from the road by narrow yards and stony drives, and through the open doorways and windows I could see the girls bending over the fine silver rings and brooches, the men and boys squatting cross-legged and carving out the wooden gods and human figures with practised certainty, and in one courtyard a couple of girls near the road tracing out the lines of the batik pattern with their little pens and tiny reservoirs of liquid dye.

Further on the taxi slowed and turned

into a long driveway screened on either side by dense shrubbery. The house was not as big as the bungalow hotels out on Sanur beach, nor as small as my old Dutch hotel in town. It was a complex of white single-storey buildings connected by covered walkways raised a few inches from the ground and open on both sides. A thick screen of palms and flowering shrubs, bougainvillaea and frangipani, hid it completely from the road and from neighbours.

I paid off the cab, stepped up to the porch and pulled the tassel of an ornately carved brass bell. Two large fat figures in stone, draped with the customary sash of incongruous black and white checked cotton, stood guard at the entrance, lifted probably from the gateway of some disused temple. Their faces wore that indeterminate smile which might be equally well interpreted as sinister, or friendly, or just plain imbecile.

The door was opened by a young servant girl in a batik blouse and skirt and a shy, wordless smile. She bowed and turned and I followed her across a cool tiled hall and through a lobby and out across one of the covered walkways to the next bungalow in the complex.

Most of this building was taken up by one big room, shaded by wide verandahs and flowering trees and cooled by an almost imperceptible buzz of air-conditioning. On the floor were delicate flowered mats that it seemed a shame to have to tramp over, and exotic draperies made the walls a riot of colour.

Round the room were lacquered tables, and cabinets and costly-looking enamelled vases with flowers. An arrangement of huge easy chairs in cane with deep loose cushions and a heavily carved teakwood table bearing a huge bowl of bougainvillaea formed the centrepiece. There was a heavy fragrance made up of the scent of the flowers, an odour of tapestry and tang of sandalwood. A dark-haired woman in a simple green dress with short sleeves and a sash sat in one of the cane chairs. A cigarette smouldered in a carelessly outstretched hand and an open magazine lay on her lap. I circled slowly round the chairs until

I stood exactly opposite her.

'Ingram,' I said, putting on my extra-special smile, the one that costs the client an extra hundred dollars.

She looked up quickly as if unaware until then of my presence, eyed me up and down, tapped ash off her cigarette into a black and grey pewter bowl, and unhurriedly placed the magazine on the table where it sat between an ice-blue Royal Copenhagen vase and a tall cut-glass tumbler holding half a pint of ice cubes and amber-coloured liquid. She was slim and not very tall, I guessed, and she had a long narrow face and big brown eyes with heavy eyelashes and very fine eyebrows behind spectacles that were faintly tinted blue. Age indeterminate: just possibly the wrong side of thirty, but I might be doing her an injustice. She took her time in replying to my greeting.

'Well, hello there,' she said eventually in a voice I recognised from the telephone. 'I'm Jacky Marczak. Andrée's friend, companion, secretary, girl Friday — call me what you will.' There was just a hint of a smile and more than a hint of bitchiness in her tone. I gave her another hundred dollars' worth of my smile, and took the chair she indicated with a flutter of well-cared for, reddened fingernails.

'What about a little drink while we wait for Andrée to put in an appearance?' she suggested brightly. 'As you will no doubt have remarked, the happy hour is already in progress. That's one thing we're very prompt about around here — no delays in getting to the happy hour.'

'Good thinking,' I replied. 'Do you keep such a thing as Bacardi, on the rocks, with fresh lime?'

'But of course, of course. Every possible comfort, even in this remote tropical paradise.'

She clapped her hands and a small man in a snow-white sarong toppled by an equally white and crisp jacket came silently through swing doors at the far end of the room. He padded silently to her chair, took the order, bowed and padded silently away. I glanced round the room at the hangings, the furniture and ornaments.

'Nice place you have here,' I said, to be

11

saying something.

'Isn't it just?' She smiled a little more, putting a lot of personality into it. 'Quite a spread, in fact. And quite old really. Andrée's folks bought it from a big Dutch merchant who made a pile out of the island's trade. That was before the war, of course, before independence, in the good old days or the bad old days, whichever way you like to look at it. Andrée's people spent a mint on doing this place up, five years ago it would be now, complete modernisation and remodelling, furniture, everything.'

'They did a good job,' I murmured.

'Yes,' she went on with a sudden excess of verve, 'pity they didn't live to enjoy it. They planned to come out here often — and then . . . that's very sad.'

'Yes it is.' I said it softly, without conviction. I'd no idea what she was talking about.

'They were killed in that San Francisco crash four years ago. I expect you remember — the plane missed the runway in the fog and went into the sea.

Only a handful survived. They were not among them.'

'No, I'm afraid I don't recall it. Must have been one of the many, many news items I've missed.'

The little man in the white sarong and jacket padded in with my drink and left again without a word. I sipped at my glass while we eyed each other speculatively.

'Miss Valence knows I'm here, I suppose?'

'Oh, sure. She'll be along. When she's good and ready.' Again I noted that little touch of bitchiness. 'You're not in a hurry, are you? No one is ever in a hurry in Bali. Why hurry? Nowhere to go, and always too damned hot to go there anyway.'

I imbibed more of my drink, the sweetness of the white rum offset by the tang of the fresh lime. I got out cigarettes and offered her one. We lit up and blew smoke at one another. She rated B− on looks, B+ on poise and style, and A− on a lithe, firm body. That was fine. Probably she didn't think I was any Valentino either. Well, that was no skin off my nose:

13

she was not the girl I had to do business with.

Through the slatted swing doors came another woman. A vision. A goddess. Swathed in a full-length brown and orange batik that was striking, that was meant to be striking. About twenty-two or three, tall, slim, and the kind of figure that you dream about, that you virtually never see outside the pages of the girlie magazines, that you think must be some kind of photographer's fraud. She had an oval face, high cheekbones, a thin and delicate nose, the mouth perhaps a little too long, the eyes dark and mysterious, the hair a rich chestnut brown. The vision swayed over to me and I grasped a soft dainty hand in my big sweating paw. I came down to earth and forced myself to concentrate. Business. I was shaking hands with a dream but a dream who was worth millions. The owner of the Balinese pearls.

The vision pronounced her name in a low, soft brown voice that matched her dress. She sat down between the Marczak and me, and the silent little man was at her side with her drink before she could look round. Some women are like that.

I ground out my cigarette and got down to the brass tacks. I tried to sound businesslike, dynamic, purposeful. I probably sounded like a moonstruck slob.

'About the pearls. I'm Harry Ingram. You got my company's cable, Miss Valence?'

'Yes, of course.' She paused to accept one of my cigarettes and I stepped over to her and got the bitter-sweet drift of her perfume while I held the lighter. 'Not so formal, please. We should be friendly about it. I will call you Harry and you will call me Andrée, if you please.'

I nodded, but I still tried to sound businesslike. 'Well, even if we're buddies and it's Andrée and Jacky and Harry or whatever, we still have to get down to details,' I growled. 'And there's no time like the present.'

'I quite agree,' she said quietly. Her voice was low with a little catch in it. As if something was bothering her and she was trying not to show it. Or perhaps it was just a mannerism. I was being much too sensitive. So I ground out my cigarette a quarter smoked and tried to sound casual.

'Do you have any idea, Miss Valence — Andrée — any idea at all, who may have stolen your pearls?'

3

'None at all, I'm afraid. None at all.'

She looked at me with steady eyes but I thought her mouth trembled for an instant and her voice had that slight catch in it again. I leaned forward in my chair.

'Let me see if I have the facts straight. According to the report I have from the insurance people, the company who ordered the investigation, the pearls disappeared two weeks ago, on the twentieth of last month. That's correct?'

'No, not quite. The twentieth was when I missed the pearls. They might have been gone some time before that. I hadn't worn them in a little while.'

'I see. But on the twentieth when you went to the safe they were not there, and the safe was intact. That much is correct?'

'Yes.'

'Who knows the combination, besides yourself?'

'Only Jacky here. But that doesn't

mean anything. You see, I'm not sure they were in the safe.' She seemed a little more self-possessed now and her dark eyes were full on me.

'I don't understand,' I said softly. 'Not in the safe?'

'Well, I often kept them in a little Japanese trinket box on my dressing table. I never gave it a thought. Security, I mean. It sounds crazy, I know, but it's so. That's the way I am, I suppose.'

'You had pearls that when last valued were assessed at over a million dollars and you kept them in a Japanese trinket box?'

She nodded.

'Unlocked, I imagine?'

She nodded again. She didn't look unhappy. She even managed a little smile.

'I know you think that's bad of me. Very silly.'

I glanced at Jacky. She sat there very still and a smile played round her mouth too. She seemed to be enjoying my reactions.

'Worse than bad,' I growled, 'it's a disaster.' I looked quickly from the one to the other of them. They were both quite

18

unmoved. It might have been only a broken mirror and seven years' bad luck.

'A disaster,' I repeated, trying to sound tough. 'You realise, I suppose, that the insurance company won't pay. Not in a million years. If the pearls had been stolen while you were wearing them — in a hold-up — or if they had been in the safe, and the safe was a good modern one, and only the two of you knew the combination and someone had cracked it — well, OK. They'd swallow hard and shilly-shally and complain and drag their feet a little. But in the end they would pay. They would have to pay — unless by some miracle I managed to recover the pearls. But not now, not like this — no way.'

They were still unperturbed. Andrée sighed softly and put down her glass.

'That's that, then. Goodbye one million dollars.' She smiled her little smile again. There was a long, uncomfortable silence.

Then I did my big-shot act, the one that's always getting me into trouble, the one that's irresistible when a doll is on the other end. A lush, beautiful doll. This time much more than that. Much, much more — a tropical goddess, no less.

'Well, not quite,' I said slowly. 'Chances are the pearls are long gone, off the island weeks ago. Chances are somebody's already counting his score in Singapore or Vegas or Los Angeles or wherever. But possibly, just possibly, they might be got back.'

Jacky opened her eyes wide, leaned forward. More interested, apparently, than the pearls' owner.

'How?' she asked, 'how could you get them back?'

'We could try advertising in the local paper,' I said. 'Offer a reward. You haven't done that I imagine. It's worth a try. Not too much, maybe twenty-five thousand rupiah and no questions asked. If the thief is an amateur, doesn't know their value, it might seem like a good deal.'

'We could try it,' Andrée murmured quietly.

'By the way, how did the thief get in? Were there windows open?'

'At night I often turn the air-conditioning off and sleep with the big doors open,' Andrée said. 'It's fairly high up here. We are actually on the slope leading up to Penelokan, the volcano you know. It can get quite cool at night. And sometimes at night I leave the room to get a drink of water. Anyone could hide in the garden and slip in while I was out of the room, or even while I was asleep for that matter.'

I nodded. 'But only the pearls went. That suggests whoever took them knew something about their value.'

'I suppose so.'

'And who did know the value of the pearls?'

'Oh, several people. Friends. They all knew about them. It was a subject of conversation when I wore them because I wore them so rarely.'

'And the servants? One of them could have taken them, I imagine?'

'It is possible, of course. But not probable. They have all been here for years. They were very fond of my parents when they used to spend time here, before . . . before the accident.' There was the catch in the voice again. Quite distinct this time.

'Did they know how much the pearls were worth?'

'No, I think not. Though they knew about the safe, naturally.'

'The fact you kept the pearls only in an unlocked box might be good from that point of view,' I said. 'They wouldn't think they were particularly valuable. Could I see the room, and the box, too?'

'Of course.'

She led the way through the swing doors at the far end of the room and down a hallway from which other doors opened. Beyond were two more open passageways, each leading off at an angle to a further part of the complex. We took the one on the right hand and came to a corridor opening on to two bedrooms and their associated bathrooms. Her room was large and airy with hangings ceiling to floor, furnishings and bed all in a soft shade of pastel blue, and big French doors opening to a covered verandah. She was right. If the doors were open anyone could slip in and out in a moment. Even if the doors were shut, getting in would be only a matter of seconds. A very easy room to get into. There was a carved teakwood dressing table, fellow to the table in the sitting-room, and on it sat the Japanese trinket box, lacquered in black and gold, surrounded by the usual scatter of little pots and bottles that women always have on a dressing table.

I opened the box — no lock, as I'd supposed — and looked quickly through a jumble of chains and brooches. All costume jewellery, paste, diamanté, nothing that looked worth very much. I closed the box again. Andrée went over to the far wall by the bed and drew aside the hangings. There was the safe. Not new, but not so old either. And very obviously intact. I nodded and she let the hangings fall back into place. Jacky stood in the doorway observing it all. She was wearing that mischievous little know-it-all smile again.

'The pearls were in the box with these other things?' I asked.

Andrée nodded. 'Yes, but I kept them separately, wrapped in a piece of green felt. The felt went too, with the pearls.'

'Tell me about the pearls. What did they look like?'

'A string of huge South Sea pearls.' She wrinkled her brow as if she had difficulty in remembering. 'Rather chunky. Twenty-five of them, set in some fine gold open-work with small rubies in between. The pearls themselves are really big, somewhat irregular in shape, as the South Sea pearls are. Some people might think them ugly. It was not so much their size, it was their age which made them valuable. The necklace is associated with one of the royal houses of Bali. They were originally an heirloom of a local princess in the 1880s. And much older than that because they came into her family as a wedding gift, I think as far back as the fifteenth century.'

I nodded. 'Then they must be easy to identify and that makes the piece difficult to sell, at least as a whole. Whoever took it would break it up and sell the individual pearls, although each would be worth much less, considered separately. The insurance company are sending me a photograph. I will be able to get a good idea from that, supposing we are lucky enough to see them again.'

We walked back, the three of us, to the big sitting-room and I took her soft hand for a moment. She panicked me again with those dark unfathomable eyes. In another minute I would say or do something really stupid.

'I'll see about the advertisement' was what I did say, as calmly as I could. 'And I will be in touch. Don't be too hopeful, it's a very long shot. In the meanwhile we must try the other tack. I will need a list of all the people who have been in the house recently, say in the last six weeks. Have it ready for me for tomorrow. Names, addresses, background — anything about them that might be relevant. Especially whether you know they are in some kind of financial trouble.'

She nodded and looked away as if she didn't want to meet my eyes. That was the first time she'd done that. I wondered about it. I wondered about it all the way back to the hotel and while I sat over my beer and *rijstaffel* in the hotel dining room. About half-past ten the waitress called me to the phone. It was Jacky Marczak.

'Andrée forgot to tell you one little thing,' she said breathily.

'Yes?'

'Yes. She kept the pearls in the Japanese box only recently. Only in the past few weeks.'

And she rang off.

4

The next day was bright and blue and every bit as steamily hot. I had a solitary, lazy swim in the pool before breakfast, showered, shaved, dressed, ate my bacon and scrambled eggs and was still down in the newspaper office bright and early.

Next I rang the house to see if the list I'd asked for was ready. A man's voice answered, the manservant of yesterday, I guessed. Both the ladies were out. They had left no list, no message. But he could tell me where the ladies had gone. They had gone to the Barong dance.

The Barong dance. When a million in pearls was at stake. The girl at the desk told me where the dance was being given, and a taxi had me there in fifteen minutes. The terrace before the temple served as the stage and the various characters in the dance entered down a flight of stone steps set in the middle. Near relations of my fat friends of yesterday sat on guard either side of the steps garbed in the same black and white checked cotton. On the far side of the terrace squatted the gamelan orchestra: twenty men and boys, two with drums and the rest with little hammers in their hands, striking their odd assortment of gongs of all shapes and sizes just at the right moment, the plaintive metallic music rising and falling with elusive repetitions of themes that were hard to remember — no music, no conductor; without effort, without concentrating, playing the pieces they had learned as children and performed a thousand times. The courtyard in front of the temple was filled with chairs and packed with people, mainly tourists, who craned to see every movement of the dancers and flashed their cameras and swung their cinés incessantly. The Barong himself was on the stage, prancing about with a couple of comic characters in gorgeous costumes and heavy, obviously fake, moustaches, surrounded by a score of lithe young men armed with kris.

I squeezed into a standing space and

spotted my party straight away. With Andrée and Jacky was a strapping, good-looking lad, about twenty-six or twenty-eight, six-foot-three and shoulders in proportion, blond wavy hair and bright blue eyes. As handsome a piece of hulking manhood as an impatient virgin could dream of. Andrée was giving him the business with little asides whispered in his ear and sidelong glances through half-closed eyes. And he responded with flashing teeth and a grin as smooth and insincere as Don Ameche's in one of those old-fashioned Hollywood musicals, the ones where everyone smiles constantly through all the misunderstandings and the banalities of the plot never prevent the show from going on. I knew instinctively I was not going to like this character.

I caught them as they left the temple lagging behind all the clacking, camera-happy folks from the tourist mini-buses.

'Hello, Harry,' Andrée said casually, 'how nice to see you' — as if it was the most natural thing in the world we should meet by chance at a Balinese Barong dance. She picked up my glance at the blond he-man. 'Oh, let me introduce you to an old friend, Carl, Carl van der Pohl. Carl does all kinds of exciting things in the jungles of Sumatra. Isn't that so, Carl?'

And she threw him one of those sidelong glances that should have had him panting. All he did was give me a shot of his Don Ameche grin, only close-to, showing teeth that could have been sold to a toothpaste advertising agency, crush my hand in a paw that was probably used to throttling Sumatran tigers, and say 'Hi, nice to meet you' with a powerfully guttural accent in a way that suggested the opposite.

He turned to Andrée. 'Let's go get a drink at the hotel, honey. And maybe cool off in the pool afterwards.'

'Why not?' she smiled back. 'Jacky, be a darling and go find the horseless carriage, would you?'

The Marczak hurried off crying 'Don't you go away now. It should only take me an hour to get that heap disentangled from the five hundred others.'

In fact she was back very quickly, looking cool and important in a big air-conditioned white Mercedes that appeared grotesque among the crowd of cycles and motorbikes, like a duchess who'd got by mistake into the servants' quarters. It took a little time to thread the big car through the traffic and over to Sanur and Carl's hotel, the Bali International, a space that Andrée and Jacky filled with small-talk about the dance while I smoked and pretended not to take any notice of Carl, who smoked too, and smiled and shot an occasional glance at me which said all at once that he wasn't sure why I was there, he didn't like my being there, and who the hell was I anyway?

In the hotel bar we gave the other customers the benefit of more of our small-talk, and after a long while Andrée and her blond god decided to go swim. Jacky and I finished our cigarettes and strolled out past the pool and through the scatter of trees out on to the beach itself. The sand dipped down to a shallow lagoon cut off by a reef from the open sea beyond, and in the distance native fishing boats were drawn up high on the beach with their sails flapping in the hot breeze. A few people lounged by a clutter of stalls selling the usual array of multi-coloured batiks and wooden carvings of the island deities, Siva, the Garuda bird, wrinkled old fishermen with nets over their shoulders, and voluptuous naked women with improbably jutting breasts, all stained the same uniform dark brown with Kiwi-brand boot polish.

The two of us kicked our way through the sand and took possession of a couple of convenient chaises-longues. We lay there a long time listening to the water lap quietly on the beach and feeling the sun burn our faces.

'And what do you make of the boy friend?' she asked at last.

I shrugged my shoulders and pursed my lips at her. 'Seems OK,' I grunted, 'if you like them tall, strong and handsome. Could be the answer to some maiden's prayer.'

'And some non-maiden's, too,' she replied tartly. 'A big hunk of meat with too little to justify his own good opinion of himself and not too much on top — that's how I rate him. She's throwing herself away on a guy like that.'

'Her business, I suppose,' I put in. There was more silence. Then I said irritably: 'Is he on the list? The list of visitors I asked for, that's not been produced as yet?'

'And how. Right at the top,' Jacky grunted, ignoring my crack about the list. 'He's always hanging around. And when he's not in the house she's over here.'

'Nice work if you can get it,' I remarked softly.

'And you can get it if you try,' she chuckled. 'I know that old number too.'

We grinned at each other, a little more friendly.

'He lives here permanently, does he? Must be a little expensive.'

'Sure. Puts on the style, don't you know.' She turned her head away and looked quiet and thoughtful. 'Expensive I guess is right. He may have a deal going with the management — free board and lodging in return for services to the guests. Like chatting up the old ladies — wouldn't they love that? — and escorting the younger ones around, the single ones who thought this was some sort of tropical Coney Island with palm trees and feel kind of in need of protection — they'd love that too. And organising parties and telling them all about the Ramayana dances and making up a foursome at bridge — all that jazz.'

'You must admit he has the equipment for it.'

'Yes he has. But on the other hand,' she went on, 'he maybe pays his own way. He made some money a while ago in Sumatra.'

'Then he's not likely to have taken the pearls.'

She smiled at me a little sharply at that. 'I guess not,' she murmured slowly. 'But that was a while ago that he made the money and he enjoys spending it.'

'He may be running a little short by now?'

'It's possible. I've no idea how much he made. And he's never gone back.'

'To Sumatra? How did he make money there?'

She turned on her side towards me, curled herself up small and used her left hand to shade her eyes from the sun.

'He was part of a surveying team that went out into the jungle prospecting the soil and minerals. Some scheme sponsored by the UN to see if there was land worth cultivation, feed the hungry millions of Indonesia. But I guess he found something more valuable than potential farm land. I know these soil analysts and development eggheads can make a pile of dough on a tough assignment, and I guess it was plenty tough living in the jungle for six months. But I reckon he made a lot more than his salary.'

'I see. A little mysterious is he? And then he just spent it?'

'I don't know. Never bothered to find out. You really want to know?'

'Well, let's say you've aroused my curiosity. A man who likes to live in style, then perhaps runs out of cash — '

'You think he could have taken the pearls? Carl? Really?'

And a little tip of pink tongue licked round her carmine lips. It was an idea that appealed. Yes, it was an idea that appealed to her very much.

'Carl,' she mused. Then after a pause: 'I think I know how to find out more. Yes, I think I know how to find out more.' And her eyes narrowed and her lips closed and clamped tight.

'More about him, and about anyone else who seems to fit the bill,' I growled in a matter-of-fact way. 'And do you think you could hustle up Andrée on that list? I must have the information if I'm to do any sort of job on these pearls.'

'Sure, I'll light a squib under her tail right away. But I don't promise results. Andrée will do things in her own way in her own time. She's a law unto herself. She's not a gal to be rushed. No sir.'

'Well, OK,' I croaked irritably. 'She likes doing things her own way. But she doesn't seem to realise how badly I need the information. I'm just wasting time kicking my heels around here, and my time costs money.' I paused and let the irritation drop out of my voice. Then I said quietly: 'In fact I almost get the impression she's not very concerned about the pearls. As if she doesn't mind losing a million dollars. Or as if . . . as if, almost, she hadn't really lost them at all . . . even knows where they are all the time.'

I watched her face to see what this did to her. Not much. She raised her eyebrows a fraction and smiled at me innocently.

'You know,' she said very softly, 'I get exactly the same idea.'

5

Back at my hotel I ate a late snack in lieu of lunch and sank an ice-cold beer. It was clean and fresh after the gin and the hot sun and glaring sand of the seashore. I went to my room, stretched out on the bed and tried to think it over. There wasn't much to go on. Only words, hints, suspicions, the tone of a voice. What I'd said to Jacky was true: Andrée didn't seem worried about losing the pearls. Of course, that might be just her way, her attitude to life. Or the insulating effect of having an awful lot of money. I wouldn't know about that. But all the wealthy people I'd ever met had seemed to be money-conscious, as if they still had it to make and couldn't stand a loss. What had Jacky said? That she liked to do things in her own way in her own time. She was certainly playing the pearls very cool, very cool indeed. It had me wondering.

I gave up the wondering and cooled off

my frustration in another lazy swim. I had the pool to myself and I swam slowly up and down savouring the almost frigid wetness against the sticky heat of the world beyond the water. After a long while I climbed out and found a canvas lounger in the sun. I was cool enough and wet enough to welcome the sun for a little while. A tall, strongly built man emerged from the hotel and walked over to where I lay. Tall and light in colour for a Balinese, I thought. Smartly dressed, too, in a freshly-cleaned and pressed white tropical suit, white shirt and dark tie with little red diamonds on it.

'Mr Ingram, I believe,' he said politely with very little trace of accent. 'Please excuse my intrusion. My name is Peter Vetran. You do not know me, but I think I can be of service to you.'

I stared up at him from the lounger. From where I lay he looked enormous.

'That depends,' I said, 'on what you have to sell. I don't need a nice girl, I'm not interested in boys, I've had my fill of temple dancing and I'm not in the mood for having my fortune told.'

He laughed good-humouredly. 'No, Mr Ingram, you mistake me. I'm not selling any of those things. Only one thing. Information.'

I stared up at his broad, slightly sallow face and wide friendly smile. He might be thirty, thirty-five, and he looked durable.

'I don't see how you know what information would be of interest to me.'

'Let me hazard a guess, Mr Ingram. Pearls. What about pearls?'

'Pearls,' I repeated softly, without expression.

'Yes, pearls. Let me be more specific. Missing pearls.'

'I don't see how you would know about missing pearls. Unless it was you who stole them.'

He laughed again, a very pleasant, cheerful sort of laugh. 'You will have your little joke, Mr Ingram. No, I did not steal them. Had I done so I would hardly be here talking to you now.'

'Perhaps not. But then again, perhaps yes.'

'But if I could give you some information, Mr Ingram,' he was serious now, 'and if my information led you to the pearls, I think you would be prepared to pay handsomely for my services?'

'Oh, handsomely.'

'We are talking about a great deal of money, are we not? Many thousands of dollars? Many, many thousands of dollars?'

'Probably. If your information really led to the recovery of the pearls, there would be a very large reward. But the point is, what information do you have?'

He smiled again. 'You are very businesslike, Mr Ingram. I like that, I think we could do business. However, I am not yet quite ready to divulge my information.'

'Ah.'

'Perhaps you think you can find the pearls yourself, without my help. I do not think you will succeed, but of course you will want to try. In a few days you will see that you need help, my help. You will need my help and so I give you my card and I await your call. In a few days.'

He placed the card on the little wooden table beside the lounger and strode off.

He was gone before I could pick up the card. What it said didn't help me very much: 'PETER VETRAN, Djalan Pasar 136. Telephone 362'.

I took the card with me to my room and put it away in my wallet. I showered and changed and tidied up a little and sat down in the one easy chair, and I thought about it all the time I was doing these things. Outside the light grew softer and the evening grew quiet and peaceful.

The telephone rang. The sober voice of the sober girl at the desk told me that a lady was waiting for me outside in a car. I didn't need to ask if it was a big white Mercedes, but I wondered about the girl. It was the Marczak, changed into a flimsy floral blouse and white pleated skirt and her hair all freshly done and a big smile on her carmine lips.

'Hi there. I'm going down to Kuta to see the sunset over the water. Want to come along?'

'Kind of you to come by,' I smiled back. 'I was just wondering what to do with myself this beautiful evening.'

I got in beside her and got a faint drift

of her perfume, or perhaps it was just the scent of the flowers in front of the hotel. She put on her sunglasses and eased the big car out into the traffic. In a few minutes we were out of Denpasar and on the road leading to the airport. At Kuta village we made a right and after a couple of hundred yards were on the great stretch of sandy beach. Kuta beach. Hippy paradise. Where you come for a week and stay for a year. Where you can shack up for the night for a dollar, get a girl for the same. Get a fix for not a lot more.

There was a row of women with batiks, blouses, cotton skirts, ornaments and earrings spread out on the beach. We walked along the row and Jacky asked to see a purple and black batik that had a motif of Legong dancers.

Two women shared the display and the second tried to attract away Jacky's attention. 'Buy from me, lady! Buy from me, sir!' she cried in a wheedling tone. Jacky involved herself in bargaining with the first woman. We walked on a few yards and the woman ran after us, holding out the piece of cloth and nodding her head reluctantly to the price.

Jacky paid her and we walked away. 'They always ask three times as much as they expect to get. She's still making a good price. Wouldn't have let me have it otherwise.'

We walked on over some dunes. The beach stretched away to our right, and ahead, over the sea, a great orange sun tinted the quiet water the colour of wine. All the young hippy sunbathers had gone to find food and we had five miles of beach to ourselves. We went a little further and Jacky stopped and spread out the batik on the sand. We sat there savouring the relative cool of the dusk and watching the sun sink perceptibly below the horizon, the brief equatorial sunset. Within moments it was almost dark.

Jacky turned half round and looked back at the shacks which lined the head of the beach. 'So much beauty and so much ugliness,' she commented, as if speaking to herself. 'So many aimless young lives frittering away without purpose, without any object except pleasure, the pleasure of the moment, the sheer indulgence of the senses.'

'My, we are serious suddenly,' I said. 'You know, perhaps it is they who are right and we who are wrong. They've seen what the rat-race has done to people and they've decided they want no part of it.'

'And they make a principle out of idleness and a philosophy of avoiding responsibility,' she replied tartly.

'I know. While we struggle to make an honest dollar. And what does it get us? Money to put in the bank and worry about, possessions we don't really need and that are ultimately useless, and in the end ulcers, thrombosis and cancer.'

'My God, if I'm serious, you're cynical,' she cried. 'No one would dream you could trouble your head about something so sordid as a string of pearls.'

I rubbed my chin reflectively. 'Well, that's my thing, that's how I live. I have to be concerned with matters more or less sordid. In this case, missing pearls. In another, a missing woman, who turned out to have been murdered. In yet another, emeralds, which turned out to be really heroin. And on the way some very sordid things happen, people get hurt, sometimes they die.'

'How exciting. Sudden death in the tropical paradise. Now it's my turn to be cynical.' I could see her smile in the gathering gloom. 'Making any progress on the case? No, of course not — you need that list. Oh, by the way, I talked to Andrée about it. She's promised to have it ready in the morning. I made her promise, so perhaps it really will materialise.'

'I have to thank you for that.'

'You do. So why not do it properly?'

She snuggled up close and I felt the firmness of her body. Smooth fingers insinuated themselves into mine. I half-turned on my side and now she pressed hard against me. Our lips were inches apart and she raised her head to close the gap. The pressure of her fingers increased. Her eyes were dark, fathomless pools, her eyelashes a huge black fringe of savage spikes. Our lips met for a long half-minute.

'That was good,' she murmured. 'You see, Bali does have its compensations.'

There didn't seem to be any answer to that. We kissed again, and when we came out of the clinch she lay back, stretching out on the batik. In the gloom I could just make out the pattern of Legong dancers like a halo around her head.

'You can unbutton my blouse, if you like,' she whispered.

'Not here,' I said, a little huskily, 'not in the middle of Kuta beach. We're liable to attract a highly interested audience.'

'You really are rather damn stuffy,' she said with a lot of bite in her tone. 'I suppose you need the ideal conditions, a softly-furnished dimly lighted lady's boudoir with at least a king-sized bed and crisp, clean sheets and no one, but no one, within a radius of five miles.'

'Yes, I think that would suit me. Throw in a good juicy T-bone steak beforehand, and a bottle of Beaune '77 to go with it, and by the bed a nice decanter of Scotch, Glenfiddich for preference, and perhaps a *soupçon* of Courvoisier for a nightcap.'

She laughed, whether in amusement or

in bitterness it was difficult to tell.

'You really gripe me, you really do, you sonofabitch,' she spat. Then she pulled me down and we got to it again. When I took my lips away she said softly: 'I'm a very accommodating woman, you know. I'll see what can be arranged.'

'I'll look forward to it.'

'Don't think I do this with every fresh guy who happens along,' she said with some firmness. 'It's just that . . . just that, I guess, I feel kind of sorry for you.'

'That's very good of you.'

'And there's no need to be sarcastic.'

She sat up, took a comb from her bag and began to tidy her hair, pull down her skirt where it had ridden up. 'Oh, by the way,' she said, just a shade too casually, 'I think I know of someone who might be able to help — with the pearls, I mean.'

'Ah, the pearls. They do keep cropping up, don't they? His name does not happen to be Peter Vetran by any chance?'

I could just see enough in the dark to note the sharp turn of her head. Perhaps she started, too, I couldn't be sure.

'Who? Peter Vetran? Never heard of him. Who's he?'

'Oh, just a man I ran into. Or ran into me, it hardly matters. It seems there's an awful lot of people taking interest in the pearls. Who's your someone?'

'I'll take you to see him, if you like. Right away, this evening. Why not?'

'But who is he?'

'Let's go. I'll tell you about him on the way.'

We got up off the batik and she shook it free of sand, folded it and put it under her arm. We ploughed silently back across the beach. In the car she switched on the interior light and did some more adjusting of her hair, applied fresh carmine to her lips. She took a handkerchief from her bag and used it to rub the corner of my mouth, showed me the red smear on the snow-white cambric.

'Always best to remove the evidence, you should know that.'

'Even if the detective is watching? What about the man you are taking me to see?'

'His name is Max Coffman,' she said, very matter-of-fact. 'An Australian by birth, I think, but you wouldn't know it. He spent a long time in America, knocked about all down the length of the West Coast, then spent time in the Pacific and ended here in Bali.'

'What does he do?'

'That's a good question. Not much of anything. He says he's in export- import, but I don't know what that means. I doubt if Max does either. He makes a dollar here, a dollar there. He'll tell you his life story for a couple of drinks, provided they're long ones.'

'I get the idea,' I murmured slowly in order to be saying something, 'an island drifter, doesn't do much of anything.'

'You could say that, I guess. But Max is not just a bar-lizard. He's been around and he still has a lot of style — when he can afford to put it in.'

'How does he come into the matter of the pearls?'

'Well, let's put it this way: not much goes on in Bali that Max doesn't know about. He won't waste your time, I assure you.'

She put away her bag and turned the

key in the ignition. The engine roared and then dropped to a steady purr that was comforting in the silent blackness.

'Just one last question, please, Jacky. How do you know him? What is he to you or Andrée?'

She turned and looked me full in the face.

'He's a guy who's never here but he's always around. He's a guy who sleeps when you're awake and vice versa. He's a guy who might have made it right to the top but keeps sliding back to the bottom. He's a guy very far from ignorant, and on occasion loaded with charm, who lives in a filthy back room.' Her voice kept rising as she spoke, and now she choked back what might have been a sob. 'He's a guy I was in love with once, and he's a guy who never even realised it.'

She let the brake go with a jerk and the Mercedes jumped forward and pitched away towards the lights of Kuta village.

6

She didn't say any more as the car moved slowly through the village, dodging the cyclists and pedestrians, the people who suddenly stopped and hollered to friends in a café and shouted to acquaintances across the road. A youth in a dirty sweatshirt and stained, ragged shorts staggered in front of the car holding a bottle of beer to his mouth, and with the luck of the drunk staggered away again, just in time. He was tall and blond and well-built and he reminded me of a shabby, younger version of Andrée's Dutchman. The car moved on into Denpasar and crossed the big bridge over the stream which runs through the middle of town, its murky water and garbage-strewn banks mercifully invisible in the darkness. We turned right by the market and went down a little narrow street of shuttered shops, then left into a small square where three roads met and out on the one to the right. This was a wider road with some shops still open, cafés and occasional small hotels which catered for the Indonesians and low-budget European tourists.

It was outside a hotel of this kind that Jacky stopped the car and we got out. A crumbling sign that might have been freshly painted at the time of the 1945 revolution read: 'Hotel Lavinia. Rooms for rent'. We went in through a dimly lit hallway, across cracked, uneven tiles and past a table where three men sat engrossed in some gambling game. Beyond the table was a wooden partition and then a stove on which a plump, middle-aged Balinese woman was grilling *satay*. Jacky said to her: 'Mr Coffman?'

The woman barely bothered to look up, merely pointed with her free hand and kept her mind on the *satay*. We moved towards the direction indicated, down the corridor, through an open doorway and out across a small patch of broken ground where a dog growled and moved reluctantly out of our path and chickens flapped uneasily in the background. A broken concrete pathway was illuminated by a single low-powered bulb and from the pathway a row of doors opened. None of the doors had any numbers but Jacky went unhesitatingly to the one she wanted. A man's voice answered to her knock and we went in, shutting the door behind us.

The room was something out of Somerset Maugham's stories of the South Seas in the 1920s. Light was provided by two naked bulbs and between them an old-fashioned ceiling fan turned slowly, its shaft moving with the motion and threatening to detach itself imminently. On one wall was an elderly iron bedstead with its torn mosquito net dropping above like a praying mantis. Next to it was a tiny enamelled iron washbasin, and just beyond that a door-less opening gave on to a small patch of damp concrete surmounted by a discoloured shower-rose and a length of pipe from which old rust-streaked cream paint was flaking. On the further wall stood an antiquated chest with ill-fitting drawers and a rickety upright chair that should have been part of the set of *White Cargo*. There were a few pegs for clothes and a bookcase that held some forty or fifty well-used volumes, and alongside that an incongruous modern steel and plastic stand which supported a record-player and a pile of records. The centre of the room was taken up by a substantial teakwood round table that might have been a nice piece when it was new; but that was a long time ago. Round it were three easy chairs of basket-work and in one of them a man was sitting.

He wore an old pair of white canvas shoes, or shoes that had been white once, creased and dirty white trousers, a white shirt with a tear in the shoulder, open at the neck, and a black and white silk scarf tied loosely round his neck. The scarf gave him a raffish look of the 1930s, like a survivor of the good old days at Le Touquet. He was a little above medium height, his figure and face both lean and his black hair was thinning in front and going a little grey at the temples. His face had well-marked bone structure, the eyes a little wary, the mouth thin, the chin strong. He could have made a photographer's model for trendy clothes when he was ten years younger; some people would call him plenty handsome still.

'Why, Jacky, what a pleasant surprise. I was just thinking about you,' he said in a husky baritone with a touch of American accent.

'Sure you were, honey,' she replied briskly, 'sure you were.' She bent and pecked him on the forehead. 'I've brought a friend to see you, Max. Harry Ingram. He wants to talk to you, get some advice.'

Max got up and shook hands. 'Well, that's fine, Harry. Why don't you take a seat and relax. Whisky?'

He bent and rummaged under the bed and came up with a bottle.

'Have to keep it down here,' he explained with a laugh, 'in case the woman who cleans up takes a fancy to it. Some damned unknown brand, I guess, but it makes you pie-eyed just the same.'

He found three glasses among the debris on a shelf, rinsed them under the washbasin tap and poured out three stiff jolts of the amber liquid. 'Here's to crime,' he said and emptied his glass at a swallow. He poured himself another couple of fingers and looked at the two of us expectantly.

Jacky put down her glass without touching the whisky. 'It's crime we've come to see you about, Max,' she said in her brisk, matter-of-fact tone. 'Andrée's pearls have been stolen. You know, those valuable antique ones, the Balinese pearls.'

Max eyed the whisky in his glass, rubbed the light stubble on his chin.

'Yes,' he said slowly, 'I think I heard a little something about that.'

'Harry here is an investigator,' Jacky went on, 'He has to make a report, to do with the insurance.'

'The insurance, of course,' Max murmured.

'He's trying to find out if there is any chance of getting the pearls back. That's where you come in. Got any ideas?'

Max swallowed his second drink and turned to me. 'How d'you like this dame?' he grumbled, a little thickly. 'She bursts in here, tells me about some goddam pearls and expects me to know who lifted them — just like that. Say, you're not drinking.'

I swallowed a quarter of mine to satisfy him. Jacky just swung hers around in the glass. 'Don't you have any ice or soda to dilute this jungle juice?' she demanded.

He got up and padded over to the door. 'I'll go get some.'

'Not water,' she called after him, 'I wouldn't drink the water in this hell-hole for all the pot in Bangkok.' She lowered her voice and glanced round the room. 'What a dump!' she spat out viciously. 'A miracle he wasn't wiped out by typhoid long ago.' Her voice softened. 'Poor Max, he's really low this time. But I guess he'll bounce right back up again.'

I was glancing at the books and records. A catholic collection. Beagle-hole's *Captain Cook*, and Moorhead's *Cooper's Creek* and *Fatal Impact*; some collections of Maigret, James M. Cain's *Double Indemnity* and Chandler's *Fare-well, my lovely*; one or two Alastair Macleans, Graham Greenes, Somerset

Maughams and D. H. Lawrences. And the records: *South Pacific* and Mahler's fourth; Muggsy Spanier and Richard Strauss.

'The export-import business not so hot at present?' I asked after a moment or two.

'A big fat zero,' she spat out with force. 'But he'll do a good job on the pearls — you'll see.'

Max came back with a small plastic basin full of ice cubes. Jacky took four and added them to her drink. I refrained from pointing out that they must be composed of the same water she had declined.

'Well, Max,' she cried, 'what d'you think?'

'Shucks, Jacky,' he complained, 'I'm just an amateur. Your friend here is a professional. All I can do is hang out my ears and see what gossip I can pick up.'

I butted in: 'That's something you can do and I can't. You know where to do the listening, and you can judge the reliability of what you hear.'

'What do you think I'm going to hear?'

asked Max. 'No one is going to tell me that Mr Whatsisname lifted the pearls and is just waiting to give them back for X thousand dollars. It's never as simple as that. All I can get is maybe a hint, a rumour, just possibly a name — of someone who might tell a little more provided his palm were well greased.'

'All you can do is see if there is any information to be picked up,' I agreed. 'Spend a little money, buy a few drinks, grease a few palms.'

'Sure,' said Max, 'and you'll see me right?'

'Within reason. If there is big money involved you had better check with me first. What I need to know in the first place is whether the pearls are still on the island.'

'Oh, you can bet your sweet life on that. This is a local job. It just reeks of it. You can bet your last rupiah on it.'

'What makes you so sure?'

'Do you remember that old story, *Double Indemnity*? One of the characters was an insurance claims manager. He could always tell a claim that smelt. Only he didn't have to smell it: a phoney claim always gave him a pain in the guts. It's the same with me. I get a gut feeling about it. Besides, it stands to reason. The only people who know the value of the pearls are the insurance company and Andrée's personal friends. And the friends are all island people. They would know about the pearls and they would know how they could be taken. No, the pearls are still on the island.'

'If that is true it narrows it down considerably.'

'Not so much,' Max replied thoughtfully. 'For one thing, there is a helluva lot of friends, and they come all shapes and sizes. I mean it might not be one of those who's light on dough. The motive might not be money at all. Have you thought of that angle?'

'It occurred to me,' I grinned, 'and I kicked it around for all of ten seconds and threw it out of the window. With something as valuable as these pearls it has to be money.'

'Maybe so, maybe not,' Max pondered, some fresh whisky in his glass. 'People will do things for the strangest reasons — envy, greed, jealousy, spite — perhaps for no reason at all, just on the spur of the moment, like shoplifting. Most shoplifting is done by people with quite a lot of cash in their pockets.'

'You can't shoplift from a safe.'

'The pearls weren't always kept in the safe,' said Max quietly. 'I understand she was in the habit of keeping them in a trinket box of some kind, right there on her dressing table.'

'How did you know that?' I asked, trying to keep the tension out of my voice.

'I know it along with forty other people. It was at a party at her place, must be six weeks or more. She made a joke of it, isn't that so, Jacky?' And he glanced at her for confirmation.

'That's right,' she agreed. 'It was a big party, and Andrée might have been just a teeny-weeny bit tight. It was stupid to talk about it, of course, even amongst one's friends, or supposed friends.'

Her last words hung in the air for a moment.

'And someone, right there at the party, on the spur of the moment might have just slipped out and taken them then and there?' I asked.

'The sort of thing a woman might have done,' Max murmured. 'If only to embarrass Andrée, or perhaps out of some grudge.'

We sat there and stared silently at our glasses for a long minute.

'That puts a different complexion on it,' I said at last. I finished my drink and got up. 'Well, see what you can hear. I'm in the market for information.'

He nodded and we moved to the door. 'By the way,' I said in as casual a tone as I could manage, 'do you happen to know a man called Peter Vetran?'

Max wrinkled his brow. 'Vetran? The name seems familiar. Someone I met in some bar, no doubt. If I could remember the bar I could perhaps remember him.'

He smiled disarmingly and I half-believed him.

We walked back across the stretch of humpy ground disturbing the same disagreeable dog and the same invisible chickens. The three men were still at their game in the hallway but the woman who was at the stove was nowhere to be seen. Outside the moon had come out from the clouds and the Mercedes stood white and stark. The warm night air carried on it an indefinable mixture of odours, of sweet-scented exotic flowers, of charcoal burners, roasting meat, ripe fruit and rotting vegetable waste. The road was still full of people, people who padded by on foot silently or swished by almost noiselessly on cycles or tore past with the raucous roar of a Suzuki.

Jacky dropped me at my hotel and drove off with a little wave of her hand. It was as if nothing at all had happened on Kuta beach. I went in and asked for my key. With it was an envelope. The note inside was written on lilac-coloured note-paper heavy with perfume, perfume that took me a long way from Kuta beach.

The curiously slanted script read: 'I have the list. Shall we say at ten tomorrow? Andrée'.

7

I was back beside the screen of flowering shrubs and my two fat friends in stone. Their insane grins were even more idiotic than before. The shy little girl in the batik blouse and skirt bowed and greeted me wordlessly again, but this time she led me out into the garden and across a stretch of grass and flower beds to where a large clump of bougainvillaea hid a small swimming pool. Small is a relative word. It was smaller than any of the hotel pools, but not by so much. And those pools had to provide for a multitude; this one catered only for one. She was stretched out on a thickly padded swing seat sheltered from the sun by a great flowered canopy. She wore a one-piece swimsuit in white, her hair thrown back carelessly over the edge of the seat, and one hand held a paperback, the other a cigarette.

I tried not to stare too long at the lines of her long, slim legs, the smooth curve of her hips, the richer curves of her breasts. She seemed not to hear me come, continued to concentrate on her book.

'Good reading, huh?' I asked.

She looked up and started a little.

'Gosh, is it so late?' she said. 'I was going to shower and dress before you came.'

'I'm glad you didn't.'

She smiled a little quizzical smile at that, put down her book and rang a lacquered brass bell that stood on the table by the cigarette packet and ashtray.

'Coffee?'

'Please. Black, no cream, no sugar.'

The manservant of before padded in and I glanced at her book as she gave him the order: *Rain*. I took a cane garden chair on the other side of the table.

'Somerset Maugham seems popular round here,' I commented. 'Highly appropriate for this part of the world, of course. I didn't think anyone read him any more.'

'I'm always years behind with my reading.'

'Great period value, the period of the

Malayan rubber planter, the Dutch island *controleur*, the pearling lugger. It's all gone — except the Raffles Hotel, where he used to write.'

'I've never been to the Raffles,' she said with a sudden enthusiasm, 'never even been to Singapore. And I've never been to Hong Kong or Bangkok or Manila or Tokyo or any of those exotic places. I always mean to go but I never even get started.'

'Just as well, perhaps, for the sake of your Somerset Maugham illusions. Half a century has made a big difference. Now you might be in any big city, with masses of indigestible concrete, poisonous fumes and monumental traffic jams.'

'I've always been afraid they would turn out like that. I wouldn't want my illusions shattered. As for Somerset Maugham — it's escapism, isn't it? One has to escape into the printed page. There's nowhere else to go.'

'That depends on what you are escaping from.'

The manservant came back with the tray of coffee things, made room on the table, set down the tray and poured out two cups of black. Also on the tray was a piece of lilac notepaper, the same as her note of the night before. She saw me glance at it.

'Ah, your precious list,' she cried. She picked it up and studied it. 'I haven't put everyone down. When I came to think how many people have been here over the past few weeks, why it frightened me. The list would have stretched as far as — '

'As far as Kuta beach, perhaps,' I interrupted.

'Yes.' She looked at me oddly. 'Kuta is as good a place as any for the purpose.'

'I thought I should let you know,' I said evenly, 'I was at Kuta beach last evening with Jacky. We sat on the beach and we kissed. I don't know why — maybe it was the sunset, maybe it was the hippies, maybe it was just something in the air.'

I saw her hand tense round the handle of the coffee cup.

'Really?' she said, her voice a little fluttery. 'Of course, what Jacky does for amusement is her own affair.'

'Nevertheless, in view of her relationship with you, and in view of mine vis-à-vis the pearls, I thought you should know. Then she took me to see a man called Max Coffman. You're acquainted with him, I think.'

'Yes, I know Max.'

'He thinks he may be able to pick up some information, perhaps get a line on who took the pearls. Again I thought I should ask if you have any objections to his doing that.'

'None at all. Why on earth should I?'

'Well, I had to be sure. It may cost some money. On top of my fee and expenses. If we find the pearls it can probably be swung on to the insurance people. And if a third party such as Max led us to the pearls I assume you and the insurance company would be prepared to come to some arrangement on paying a reward?'

'I imagine so. I haven't really thought about it.'

I drained my cup and put it down. 'I wish you would get round to thinking about these things. Perhaps you don't realise it, but you almost give the impression of not caring about the pearls, even of not wanting them found.'

Now she put down her cup and looked at me with composure. 'I'm sorry if that is the case.' She spoke coldly. 'I did not want to give that impression, I assure you.'

'Let's forget it,' I growled. 'The fact is you do want the pearls found and you are willing for me to go about it the best way I can — and you're prepared to spend a little money on the way.'

'I am in your hands, Harry.'

The use of my first name took me aback slightly. I'd forgotten we had established such familiar terms.

'Well, then, let's see the list.'

She handed it to me and I got the same drift of perfume from the notepaper. Perfumed notepaper is not much in my line, but on the odd occasion I come across it I think of Andrée, the beautiful Andrée, lying out there by her pool in a white swimsuit, and I get a little hot under the collar.

But now I concentrated on the list.

'This is just names,' I grumbled, 'no details.'

'I'll tell you about them,' she cried sweetly, 'all you want to know.'

'Right, let's start at the top.' I found a ball-point in my jacket ready for making a few notes in the margin. 'The first is Charles Kindleberger.'

'Oh yes, Charlie. I put his name at the top because his circumstances appear to be closest to those you mentioned.'

'You mean he's short of money?'

'Not exactly. He has a nice place on the other side of Denpasar and he lives well. He certainly entertains in style. But he is a little mysterious.'

'How, mysterious?'

'About his business, his source of income. He never talks about it, and he often goes away on trips, no one knows where, no one knows why. Indeed, he's away right now, left a few days ago, I gather.'

'But he has a permanent residence here? Been here some years?'

'That is so.'

'Then I don't think he is very likely to

have taken the pearls.'

'Oh, I am disappointed. I thought you might be able to find out more about him, something exciting.'

'He's probably just a very dull businessman,' I grunted, casually making a mark against his name. 'Next we have Mr and Mrs Van Hoorn.'

There was a pause while I offered cigarettes and we went through the business of lighting them.

'The Van Hoorns,' she repeated, waving the smoke away from her face, 'a quite elderly Dutch couple, in their seventies, I guess. Now they really are hard up. I believe they have only some pension and a little income from investments, and you know what inflation has done to those.' She paused and smoked her cigarette a little more. 'Over the past few years they've fired all the servants bar the cook, and she's kept on only because she's too old to get another job. You should just see their car — must be the oldest jalopy on the island. It almost has antique value. And Mrs Van Hoorn — she's sweet, indeed they both are — I don't think she has been able to afford a new dress in years, runs up her own or gets a woman in town to make them.'

'And what did he do, before he retired?' I interrupted.

'At one time he had a job in Sarawak — or was it Celebes? — anyway, he was a kind of local administrator for one of the princes. That was before the Dutch left. They lived in some style then, lots of servants and imported luxuries, and they have wonderful stories of stately receptions and dinners and travelling up country and all that kind of thing. Then when the Dutch went he stayed on, got some kind of job in Medan, I think, running a shipping agency. And now they have retired here to Bali. Of course they can remember what it was like before all the tourists came.'

'They don't sound likely candidates either,' I said, 'too old and not the type.'

'What type *are* you looking for, Harry?'

'Well, one never knows who will commit a major crime. Some very nasty things have been done by apparently innocent teenagers, by nice old ladies who worked for charity and fine old gentlemen with kindly faces and spotless records. But not in this case. I would guess that we're looking for someone fairly specific, someone on the make, ambitious, not very old. Perhaps someone with a chip on the shoulder, who might be envious of you, your beauty, your money, your whole life style.'

She was silent for a moment. 'There's Marina,' she said.

'Marina?' I glanced quickly down the list. 'Ah, Marina Maxwell, is that her?'

'Yes, a strange woman.'

'Tell me about her.'

She pressed out her cigarette, looked round for her robe. 'Harry, I'm getting rather hot and sticky out here. I think I'll go in and shower.'

I got to my feet. 'Shall I go or wait for you?'

'No, I won't waste your time,' she said. 'We can talk while I am changing. Come along.'

She gathered up her robe and her book and cigarettes. I followed her past the pool and along a path that led to the open

French windows of her room. Inside she put down her things while I glanced round at the innocent-looking trinket box on the dressing table, the curtain that I knew hid the wall-safe. She disappeared into the adjoining bathroom, calling out: 'Make yourself comfortable, I won't be long.'

I sat in an easy chair that was placed to command a view over the garden and get the breeze from the windows. I heard water drumming on the shower floor. The list was still in my hand and now I folded it and slipped it in my back pocket. It didn't look as if it was going to be much help. Perhaps Vetran was right, perhaps I would have to go to him in the end, find out what he knew. If he knew anything —

The bathroom door opened and she pushed her head out. I got a glimpse of smooth shoulders and the rest of her swathed in a huge bath towel. 'Oh, I forgot. You will find a bottle in the cupboard over by the bed. Pour a couple of drinks, if you will. And ring for ice.' The door closed again. I clumped over to the cupboard. There were glasses, coasters, a jigger and strainer, and several bottles, a Bell's, a dimple Haig, Jim Beam, Old Granddad, Canadian Club. I took the Jim Beam and poured two small drinks. I moved a little occasional table over to the middle of the French windows and set the glasses on two coasters. Finally I moved another easy chair to the other side of the table opposite mine. She emerged just as I finished these manoeuvres. She was in a white towelling gown and she walked casually over to the dressing table and began to comb her hair. I heard her put down her comb and move to the back of the room. I heard drawers opened, the creak of a wardrobe door.

'What did you choose?'

'Bourbon, the Jim Beam. That OK?'

'Fine,' she said. 'My night supplies, you know, just in case you're wondering. Some nights I find it hard to sleep. I start thinking, and then I know I'm never going to get to sleep, and I have to get up and get myself a drink.'

I didn't say anything. If she liked a little sleep-inducer in the night that was her business. I heard little sounds, the swish of clothes against the body, the metallic trill of a zip.

'I am not embarrassing you, am I?' she asked.

'If you mean have I ever before sat in an attractive lady's bedroom while she dressed herself, the answer is yes.'

She laughed. 'I thought I was safe in assuming that.'

She appeared suddenly and flopped in the chair opposite and reached for her drink. She was in white slacks now, with a brown and cerise silk blouse and a band of the same material round her hair. She hadn't put on any make-up.

'No ice.' It was a comment rather than a question.

'No, no ice. I thought it might give your man ideas if I ordered ice in the bedroom.'

'Oh, Abas wouldn't take any notice,' she laughed. 'He's used to my ways.' She eyed me over her glass and was suddenly serious.

'You really know very little about me, Harry.'

'I can hardly know much. I first met you less than forty-eight hours ago.'

'Wouldn't you like to know me better?'

'Are you always so friendly so early in the morning?'

'That's not an answer.' She put down her glass and came and crouched down by my chair. She held her beautiful face a few inches from mine. I got the fresh clean smell of her body, the sweet scent of her hair.

'Kiss me, Harry,' she said.

8

I pulled her over on to my lap, put my hands round her head and kissed her. I moved my lips to her cheek and then to her forehead and kissed her twice again. She put her head against my chest for a long moment. Then she pulled away from me, grasped her glass and moved away to the far end of the French windows. She stood there motionless, staring out at the palms, the splash of brilliant pink hibiscus, the riot of purple bougainvillaea.

'I shouldn't have done that,' she said tonelessly.

'Why not? I'm not complaining.'

'Don't get ideas,' she continued in the same expressionless voice. 'It doesn't really mean anything. Not a thing. I was merely trying to prove something to myself.'

'Such as what?'

'Oh, I don't know,' she sighed. 'Whatever your imagination tells you. See what I can get away with, I suppose. That I can make men fall for me, a man like you, an experienced man, almost a stranger.' She turned and stared at me with a level gaze. 'Why, I bet you would like to take me into that bed right now, wouldn't you?'

Her hand that held the glass was not quite steady. There was a slightly wild look about her eyes.

'I have to admit it's not an idea I find quite resistible.'

'Oh, don't be so damned cool about it,' she snapped. She walked behind me to the dressing table and I heard her fumble with a cigarette. It took her three attempts to get it alight. She came and sat down opposite me again and drew heavily on the cigarette. She drained the last of her Bourbon and I got up, fetched the bottle from the cupboard and refilled her glass. In a few moments she grew more calm.

'You mustn't take any notice of my moods,' she murmured at last. 'Jacky will tell you I've always been a little wild.'

'That's all right, it's forgotten, and it won't cost you any extra.'

'Bastard,' she whispered softly, and then quite normally: 'We were going to discuss Marina Maxwell, were we not?'

'That's right. I believe you used the word 'strange' about her.' She sighed again, tamped out her cigarette, sat down in the easy chair and drank a little more Bourbon.

'OK. She *is* strange. She can be sweet and she can be bitchy, she can be as nice as pie and as difficult as a mule. And she has a king-size chip on her shoulder.'

'So she has moods,' I said indifferently, 'what else?'

'I am coming to that. About six months ago her husband disappeared. She never talks about it. He was a mining engineer and went on a prospecting trip in some wild part of Borneo and never came back. That's her story. Of course, he could have got separated from his crew and got lost or drowned in a swamp or got killed by the natives. Some people say the tribes in the interior are still head-hunters.'

'That's her story. What's yours?'

'I don't think Bill Maxwell is dead. I think he went to Borneo and he

81

disappeared. But he did it deliberately, to make a getaway, to get away from her. She was very dominating and I guess he just got tired of putting up with her temper and her moods.'

'Perhaps she's not sure whether he's dead or alive,' I muttered, 'whether he left her or not. That could be a rather trying situation. In either case it doesn't signify from our point of view — ' I paused and thought about it. 'I suppose she could be short of money. But how could she dispose of antique pearls? Who else is there?'

'Well, there is Lee Schneider. Lee is a bachelor, about thirty-five I guess. A doctor in private practice. Now, he's on the make for sure, a nice guy in many ways but always with an eye for the fast buck. He specialises in nervous disorders, but most of his patients are tourists from the hotels and that's an ideal situation because anyone who stays in an expensive hotel in a place like this expects to be taken for a big fat doctor's bill.'

'And they don't stay long enough to get over being grateful for feeling better and start looking at the account.'

'That's right. They lie out in the sun too long and get sunstroke and sunburn, or they go in the sea and discover they are allergic to jellyfish stings, or they walk around barefoot and pick up some unpleasant skin trouble, or they pig themselves on Indonesian food and get stomach upsets. They get prickly heat, diarrhoea and nervous prostration, and all of these things are right up Dr Schneider's alley. He's always available with his hypodermics, his pills and his potions. He comes right to the hotel room and talks soothingly, produces an ointment that cost him fifty cents and leaves a bill for fifty dollars.'

'He has it made.'

'To a degree, yes. But he isn't satisfied. He despises these people and the complaints they bring on themselves through their own foolishness, and he despises himself for taking advantage of them. He would like to be a really big noise in some big-name clinic — the world-famous Dr Schneider. But at the same time he likes making a pile of dough with minimum effort. He hates his life here, he hates his work and he would love to get away, but he stops because he knows the easiest pickings he's ever likely to find are right here.'

'He does sound as if he might be interesting,' I said. 'Perhaps I should make a call on the good Dr Schneider.'

Andrée lit another cigarette and stood again by the French windows.

'No need to do that,' she remarked in a little while. 'I've been thinking. I should throw a little party and invite all these characters. Then you can meet them and judge for yourself. Possibly tomorrow evening, if people can make it so soon.'

'That's a good idea,' I said, getting up and moving out through the windows to the path, 'save a lot of time and legwork.' We stood face to face. 'Oh, tell me, will Peter Vetran be one of the guests?'

'Peter Vetran? Is he a friend of yours?'

'No, just an acquaintance. I wondered if you knew him. He seems to know you.'

'Peter Vetran,' she repeated, 'the name

sounds familiar. Perhaps I have met him somewhere.'

'I've heard that before, too,' I said with a grin. 'You'll let me know — about the party, I mean. And thanks for your time.'

9

He leaned against the bar of the Hotel
Bali, the inevitable drink in hand, but
much smarter, more elegant than the
time I had seen him before. He wore a
cream lightweight jacket with a pale blue
shirt and blue and white spotted cravat,
powder-blue slacks and natty cream
shoes. His hair was freshly barbered and
there was no sign of stubble on his chin.

'Hello, Max,' I said. 'How's it going?'

'Better than I expected,' he replied with
a smile, 'join me?'

I looked dubiously at the pale pink
liquid in his glass. 'What is it? This 'gin
pahit' that all Somerset Maugham's
characters drink in the Far East?'

He laughed. 'No, nor Singapore sling. I
wonder if you can still get that in the
Raffles these days? You certainly can't
here. No, it's simple old pink gin, old
boy.' He glanced round the bar area and
muttered: 'I think perhaps we had better

have these outside.'

He ordered the drinks and we took a table in the shade overlooking the pool. A few feet away was an Indonesian family with three happy young children who ran into the water, splashed one another and ran laughing back again. They were the only other people outside in the heat. We sat there watching the children with the sun sparkling on the blue ripples of the pool and dazzling on the white balconies of the rooms beyond. The setting gave an unreal quality to our conversation.

'I had a piece of luck,' Max said softly. 'I think I have a line on — you know what. Quite a promising line, in fact.'

He paused while the barman set down the drinks and returned silently to his bar. I tried the pink gin and put it down. It went better with Max's outfit than with mine.

'I'm listening.'

He leaned forward confidentially. 'Andrée has a boy friend, a young Dutch fellow called Carl van der Pohl.'

'Yes, I've met him.'

'He stays at the Bali International but

he's always hanging around her place. They have a little something going between them.'

I thought of the morning and the little something that was going between her and me, that lasted all of three minutes.

'He would be in the best possible position to take the pearls, coming and going at all hours.'

'And no doubt spending a lot of time in her bedroom,' I interrupted quietly.

Max gave a quick, slightly embarrassed laugh. 'You said it, fella, I didn't.'

He wiped the smile from his face, his eyes narrowed. 'I was only going to suggest that someone who is always around is somehow the least likely to be suspected.'

'Perhaps,' I shrugged. 'But all this is known, Max.'

'I'm coming to what isn't.' He imbibed more gin and licked his lower lip with a tip of tongue. 'I happened to find out this van der Pohl needs money, bad.' The narrowed eyes watched my reactions.

'The money he made in Sumatra has run out and now he needs a grubstake,' I commented. 'He owes money at the Bali International?'

Max shook his head. 'I don't know about that. Jacky thinks he has some deal going with the management there. Could be.'

'Yes, she mentioned that to me too.'

'No, this is something much bigger. He's been trying to raise dough all over town, and not peanuts either. I hear he's been to several of the banks, the credit companies, the big merchants and they all turned him down. And he asked for — how much do you think?' His eyes bore into mine.

'I have no idea. Perhaps twenty, thirty thousand dollars?'

'A quarter of a million, no less,' Max said, pronouncing every word separately and distinctly.

I whistled, sipped a little gin while I absorbed the figure and its significance.

'How recently was this, Max?'

'Not so long ago, and not yesterday either. I would say it was about two months ago, near enough.'

'Has he attempted to raise money very recently?'

'Not to my knowledge.'

'So, about two months ago he tried to raise a big sum of money, apparently without success. Then, not very long after, the pearls disappeared. And since then he has not tried to raise any money.'

'That's about the scenario,' Max agreed. 'It sort of slots him into the star role, wouldn't you say?'

'It's a lead,' I replied. 'I'll have to work on it. If it should turn out he took the pearls I know of someone who'll be just cock-a-hoop about it.'

'Uh-huh?'

'Yes, Jacky. I think there is rather little love lost between her and Carl van der Pohl.'

He merely shrugged, drained his drink and got up. I couldn't tell if what I had just said hit any kind of target. 'I'll be moving along,' he said quietly, 'and I'll still keep on asking around. There may be more.'

'Yes, and thanks for what you have so far.'

I watched him walk into the bar, ask for the check and leave some money on the barman's plate. He cracked a joke with a couple of men in the bar and padded through the dining room and stopped to pass a few words with a couple having lunch. Then he passed out of my view towards the lobby.

An hour and a half later I had showered and changed and had grabbed a sandwich and was on my way to Sanur. Carl van der Pohl's room at the Bali International was among the single ones placed on the far side of the pool, distant from the main block of the hotel. I checked in the bar and the lobby, glanced in the restaurants and surveyed the people lying round the pool before I knocked at his door. No reply. I knocked again and listened. I could hear the sound of water swishing on a tiled floor. I knocked again more loudly still. I was just about to rap for the fourth time when he opened the door, water running from his hair, face and legs, his middle swathed in a bath-towel. He was not so pleased to have a visitor.

'Oh, it's you, Mr Ingram. Come in, come in. Sit down, won't you?'

I noticed again his strong guttural

accent. 'Excuse me, I was in the shower. I always take a shower after a swim.'

He retreated to the far end of the room where there was a wardrobe and dressing table and he began to rub himself down, comb his hair.

'I am sorry to intrude, but it would be useful if I could talk to you.'

'Certainly,' he barked, 'but I regret I can spare only a very little time. I have arranged to take a little party of hotel guests on an excursion this afternoon, to Besakih — the great mother temple of Bali, you know.'

'I won't hold you up,' I conciliated. 'We can talk while you are getting ready, if you don't mind answering one or two questions, that is.'

'Of course not. Fire away.'

'I am investigating the loss of the pearls — I am sure Andrée has told you — and of course I am interested in speaking to her friends, especially her close friends. You don't have to answer if you do not wish to.'

'I've said it's OK.' There was more than a trace of irritation in his voice. I watched him select a white T-shirt from a drawer and a pair of brown slacks from the wardrobe and start putting them on.

'I don't want to embarrass you,' I carried on, 'but my questions have to do with money. It has come to my knowledge that some little time ago you were making efforts to raise money, a very large amount of money, I understand. And that you were not successful.'

He laughed, somewhat mirthlessly. 'So that makes me your prime suspect?'

'It means you have both the opportunity and the motive.'

He finished dressing now and came and lounged opposite me on the bed. He was big and handsome all right, with that fetching Don Ameche smile when he chose to use it. I wondered how many of the lady guests on his trip would be fancying him before the day was over, would like to take his arm to climb the long flights of steps at Besakih.

'Your sources did not tell you why I wanted money?'

'No.'

'Then I will enlighten you. At least up

to a point. You know, I suppose, that I have spent some time in Sumatra. During the expedition there I made an important discovery. There were a few days when I was detached from the main camp doing some separate work on my own. I discovered a lode of a very valuable mineral — I need not tell you what. I discovered it on my own and only I know exactly where it is.'

He glanced at the large gold watch on his wrist. 'As I said, I can spare very little time. But to complete my explanation, the difficulty is that in order to exploit my discovery much money is needed. For an expedition in the jungle to examine the site more thoroughly and establish its limits; for getting in mining equipment and making a track for trucks to get in by; for bribing officials and many other necessary things. The ultimate profit will be very great, but so is the initial outlay. For the moment I have to abandon it.'

'The pearls would meet the cost, I imagine.'

He laughed, again without mirth. 'Oh, yes, of course — if I were a crook, and if I were not in love with Andrée.'

'There is that of course,' I murmured.

'And if I ever thought of taking the pearls — how do you think I could dispose of them?'

'You might not have to dispose of them. You could use them as security. But there is something else, too. Since you and Andrée are so close why not ask her to put up the money? I should have thought it was the sort of scheme that would appeal to her, especially with you as the entrepreneur and leading beneficiary.'

'Do you believe I did not think of that? Evidently there is something more you do not know, Mr Ingram. Andrée is a very wealthy woman, yes. But at present only in terms of income. All her capital is tied up, very carefully tied up — her parents saw to that when they made their wills. She cannot touch a cent of the capital until she is twenty-five, and that is more than two years away. I suppose they wanted to make sure she was old enough to know what she was doing before the money came into her hands. And to guard against her falling for some unscrupulous adventurer who would marry her just for her money.'

He was perfectly right. This was news to me. It was something I should have looked into.

'I suppose they were thinking of someone like me,' he went on, a little bitterly. 'I am not of good family, I do not have an inheritance. But I make my own money and I do not live on any woman. And . . . besides, I love her.'

'That alters the case a little,' I conceded. 'But she must still have a very big income and she can do what she likes with that.'

'It is not as big as you may suppose,' he growled. 'The lawyers in America who manage the estate are careful to take a big slice, and the taxes take another. And of course there is the establishment here to run.' He glanced at his watch again. 'I must really ask you to excuse me. I should be on my way to Besakih right now.'

I went to the door and opened it. The heat and the sunshine surged in against the soft lights and the cool of the air-conditioning. 'Thank you for talking to me,' I said, 'and for your frankness.'

I threaded my way through the throng surrounding the pool. I felt ridiculously overdressed in the middle of so many scanty bikinis and bare hairy chests. Corpulent men in striped swimshorts sat in deck chairs swigging beer and throwing their cigarette ends behind them into the flower beds. And flabby, white-skinned women lay face down on beach towels, the straps of their tops unhooked to ensure the sun reached every inch of their oil-smeared, reddened backs.

All the way back to Denpasar I thought about what van der Pohl had said. A red-hot scheme for making a killing in Sumatra, and for that all he needed was a pile of money. He couldn't raise that sort of money himself, and neither could Andrée, not before she reached the ripe old age of twenty-five. That was only two years hence, but two years would seem a long time in the circumstances. What circumstances? Well, that he was young and ambitious, and that if he was going to marry her he wanted it to be on fairly equal financial terms. Yes, the Sumatra project would be really urgent for him. All the more reason then why he might have taken the pearls. With or without her consent. Now that was something else; the pearls were an asset that was already in her hands. She might not be empowered to sell them, but they could easily be used as I had suggested, as security. It should not be too difficult to raise a quarter of a million on them if his scheme held water, if it was genuine.

The telephone in my room was ringing as I unlocked the door. Her voice was a little distorted by the crackles on the line, but it was still easy on the ear.

'This is Andrée.'

'Remarkable. I was just thinking about you.'

'Oh . . . were you?' She was just a trifle disconcerted. 'I was . . . I was wondering whether you were busy this evening.'

'Well, I have a date with Jane Fonda, but I can cancel.'

'I'm so glad,' she laughed. 'Anyway, she's much too radical for you.'

'Think so? Let me tell you I've handled women who made her look like Shirley Temple Black.'

She laughed again. 'We'll come by your hotel about seven and pick you up. Oh, by the way, it's a party on some big yacht at Singaradja. I hope you'll enjoy it.'

10

The Mercedes arrived promptly at seven. A young Balinese I had not seen before was at the wheel and I got into the spare seat beside him. The two ladies sat beautiful and relaxed in the back. Andrée had on a sky-blue gown, bright with little yellow flowers and a swathed top which left one brown shoulder bare. Jacky favoured a frothy confection with frills in pink tulle. We made small talk and tried to be witty and clever as the car moved north west out of Denpasar and then turned due north, soon passing the princely temple of Mengwi. A little further on we had left behind all but the occasional motorbike and small truck and began to climb towards the gap through the volcanoes which make up the core of the island. The air became noticeably cooler and the two women shivered under their wraps.

We had reached the lovely high lake at

Beratan before I touched on the object of the journey. Singaradja was a little port on the northern coast, former capital of the island. Jacky explained that our host was a wealthy German. He spent his days drifting about the Indies in his ocean-going yacht, had been around for a few years, but neither Andrée nor Jacky, I gathered, had ever met him before. On this occasion he had been in harbour at Singaradja for some time and had issued two previous invitations but Andrée had put him off. Carl was not enthusiastic to go, Andrée explained. It was a long and slow trip over the mountains and he didn't care for Germans — they were often so dull, arrogant and boorish. And this evening, as I knew, Carl was busy, escorting the hotel guests to Besakih, at the foot of Gunung Agung, not very far to the east of our road. He would be well on his way back by now, would have finished off the tour with a quick view of the ancient court of justice at Kelungkung, and be whiling away the last few miles to the hotel with exciting stories about the jungles of Sumatra.

So I was the substitute escort. Andrée had not enquired how I liked Germans.

'What about this mysterious yachts-man,' I enquired, 'does he have a name?'

'He calls himself Hermann Zahl,' Jacky said quietly, 'but that is probably not his true name. Rumour has it that he changed it a long time ago and before it was something entirely different.'

'Intriguing,' I remarked. 'Maybe he's the last of the untraced Nazis, the one who got away with all the loot.'

'Not old enough,' Jacky snapped shortly, 'he's about fifty, I'm told, and Hitler died in his bunker in 1945.'

'Your modern history is admirably accurate,' I grinned. 'But people who change their names either have an unfortunate one like Hickenlooper or Frankenstein, or else they have something more important to hide. Maybe he's a retired vice king from Hamburg.'

Jacky didn't smile. 'No one knows how he made his money,' she replied in a cold tone, 'but if he did make his money that way it is more likely to have been in Las Vegas than Hamburg.'

'And all he has to do,' I went on, 'is decide where he's going to sail next, raise his hook in one tropical paradise and drop it in another. Some guys have it made.'

'He usually spends several months in Bali,' Andrée put in. 'His wife is a Balinese. She is said to be very beautiful.'

'The man has discrimination as well as dough.'

'Oh, I don't know,' Jacky said testily, 'the women here soon lose their charms. They age quickly, they become gross and unattractive or skinny and wrinkled: they don't have the staying power of the white woman. And besides, they are not often well-educated or travelled or experienced. Intellectually they are very limited.'

'Depends what you're looking for,' I commented, 'it's not every guy who wants to live with a temperamental Gertrude Stein or a sexless Virginia Woolf. Some would put more weight on simplicity, good humour, and contentedness.'

We left the argument there. The car came into the little town of Singaradja, turned towards the harbour and came to rest by a wooden jetty. We walked carefully along uneven planking fitfully lit by an occasional lamp swaying in the sea breeze. There were a number of small fishing boats, then a sprinkling of larger pleasure craft. The big yacht was at the extreme end where the water was deepest. It was moored stern-on, and a smart varnished gangway with a very white hand-rope led steeply from jetty to deck. The floodlit gangway illuminated also the name painted in black letters on the transom: *Undine*.

He was almost too much the typical cartoon German, big, heavy and paunchy, with a bold, square face and short-cropped, fair spiky hair going thin and a little grey. His wife was almost his precise opposite — slim and petite, with black hair combed back into an elaborate arrangement on one side of the head, fragile shell-like ears that were almost transparent, almond eyes and delicate nose and mouth, the whole cast of her features immobile and serene, revealing nothing. One might believe that behind the beautiful mask lay deeply concealed emotion or simple nothingness — either was possible. She wore an elaborate Balinese sarong and tunic in deep blues, browns and black, and sandals of fine golden strands decorated her tiny bare feet. She wore an array of jewellery, rings, bangles and necklace, which on her was quite natural and in perfect taste.

Zahl led us forward in single file by the narrow strip of open deck between the saloon and the rail. The guests were gathered on the fo'c'sle, some dozen people who did not quite fill the narrowing space between the converging rails, the gaps between the ventilators, clews and anchor gear. Hard at the foot of the bridge was the bar table, covered by a white cloth, and a steward in black trousers and starched white jacket buttoned up to the neck supervised the array of bottles. Over everything was stretched a canvas awning designed to protect against midday sun and late afternoon showers, but now creating a sense of enclosure and privacy.

On the port side the moon lit a path across the ripples of the harbour and turned the water into a silvery grey. There was an occasional stir of the vessel against the slack of her moorings and just enough movement to remind one that this was a ship, with fifteen feet of sea water beneath it.

We were formally introduced to the other guests, principally local people, government officials and the like. There was a friendly middle-aged Australian couple, retired sugar-planters from Queensland, who told me about the toads, big as small dogs, that inhabited the sugar canes and sometimes invaded the house; a somewhat aloof Danish pair, both tall, slim and blond, who came from one of the other yachts in the harbour; and a single English girl who was working her way around the world. She had spent some months on a kibbutz in Israel, worked as a secretary in Durban and a nursemaid in Calcutta. She was fresh from a job in Australia where she had been a waitress and general help on a remote so-called sheep station that had highly alkaline water and made money by feeding tourists travelling in campers and Dormobiles. Bali disappointed her, she said. Among all the tropical extravagance of brilliant green rice-paddies, palm trees and exotic flowers, there was so much squalor and so much poverty, and not a little disease. She had gone about the island eating in native restaurants and sleeping in primitive native hotels. The tourists cosseted in their air-conditioned luxury never even noticed the truth: the minibuses whisked them from hotel to temple and back to their interrupted gin and tonics. Their utmost adventure was to bargain feebly with a street-seller for a batik or painting or carving. No, not a tropical paradise. I had moved on among the other guests before I thought to ask how she had come to be on Hermann Zahl's *Undine*.

Andrée was alone in the bows, staring out at the moonlight on the sea.

'Beautiful night. May I refill your glass?'

She looked quickly at me and turned back to the sea. 'Beautiful night, beautiful yacht, beautiful party, beautiful people,' she sighed.

'What is that meant to be,' I asked, 'appreciative, sardonic or merely bitchy?'

'Something of each, I suppose. One should be deliriously happy, of course, enjoying the good life, the luxurious life of the élite. But sometimes it all seems terribly unreal. All that money does is provide an insulation from the happiness — and the misery — of the world that exists beyond.'

'You should talk to the English girl,' I said, 'the young one in the white — exactly her sentiments.'

'I haven't met her. I saw you speaking with her. Attractive, isn't she?'

'I hadn't thought about it. I was listening to what she had to say. But I suppose she is, in a typically English, healthy, fresh-complexioned kind of way.'

'Not beautiful, like me?'

'No.'

'Put your arm around me, Harry.'

'OK — and to hell with the scandal.'

'Please don't joke about it. I really want an arm around me.'

'Any arm?'

'Tonight, yours.'

I put my arm around her and felt her shiver. She continued to shiver as I held her, nestling close to me. The breeze off the sea was cool now, but not that cool. I was dimly conscious that eyes turned towards us, glances were exchanged. The Balinese would be saying among themselves: 'Oh, these uncivilised westeners, how they have to display their feelings in public!' Why should I care? I had in my arm the most beautiful woman on this yacht, on the whole damn island, possibly the whole of south-east Asia — not overlooking the hostesses on Singapore Airlines.

'I think we had better return to the here and now,' I said after a few moments. 'After all, there are more than the two of us.'

She didn't reply for so long I thought she hadn't heard me. Then she sighed again: 'A pity. Circumstances are never right for us, are they Harry?'

'There could be better places and times, if you wanted to find them.'

She made no reply as I turned her in my arm, released her and saw her stroll straight over to the nearest knot of people and start into what looked a care-free, high-spirited conversation. I clumped to the bar and got another drink. Scotch, the best. I emptied that and then another. Jacky was looking at me disapprovingly. To hell with women. I downed another Scotch just to spite her. I got myself another glass and went over and dazzled a diminutive island administrator with my vast knowledge of his problems of population explosion, overcrowding and food resources; I startled the friendly Queenslanders by the extent of my familiarity with the somewhat modest delights of downtown Brisbane; I reminisced with the two aloof Danes about the Tivoli Gardens of remote Copenhagen, the Stroget — the sex shops that were much exaggerated, they said — the Royal Danish opera and ballet, and the famous store, *Illum*; I talked Suez, Calcutta, Bangkok and Singapore with the English girl — they were all vastly over-rated, she said firmly. And I drank more whisky. The Scotch was doing things to me. I was way over my limit and

I didn't care. I was gay, wild and happy, and the last thing I had on my mind was a million dollars' worth of pearls.

The big German loomed in front of me and blocked out with his bulk six guests and half the harbour. His big square face was unnaturally large, his voice unbearably loud. I could see as if under a microscope the great glistening beads of perspiration on his forehead.

'I hope, Mr Ingram, you are enjoying my little party,' he said politely.

'A great party,' I grinned, patting his arm patronisingly, 'the greatest. I haven't enjoyed myself so much since I was thrown out of a Richard Burton-Elizabeth Taylor binge in Acapulco.'

'Acapulco, ah Acapulco,' he said dreamily, as dreamily as a big, fat, middle-aged German can get. 'I have been there, Mr Ingram. As beautiful a place as any lapped by the waters of the ocean.'

His guttural accent reminded me of someone else, someone I had talked to years ago — or was it only that afternoon? — yes, that was it. And I didn't like him any better.

'Ja,' he said emphatically, 'Acapulco and Malibu and Carmel and Palm Beach and Rio. All are beautiful, but not the same as the East.'

'You're absolutely right,' I agreed thickly, 'nowhere is like the East.'

'Ja, I prefer the East — Penang, Macassar, Timor, Apia, Tahiti. The South Seas, the swaying palms, the coral reefs, the blue lagoons and the pearl fishers. Have you seen the pearl fishers at work, Mr Ingram?'

His words came to me as from a great distance, from the end of a vast echo chamber. His face was thrusting into mine. I could even smell the perspiration now. I tried to pull myself together. 'I've seen Bizet's opera, *The Pearl Fishers*,' I murmured in total irrelevance, 'marvellous score, but the piece is set in ancient Ceylon.'

He smiled at me sympathetically, and went on as if I hadn't spoken. 'It is a wonderful sight, Mr Ingram. Imagine those slim brown bodies plunging down to the bottom of the lagoon in search of the pearl oysters. It is truly remarkable the amount of time they can stay below the surface, and just when you think they must drown up they come with an armful of shells. And then to see the fellows in the boat prise open the shells with great sharp knives and prod for the pearl. Then imagine the pearl, an object of beauty that began as a mere irritant, an alien body in the oyster, a minute worm, the merest speck of sand. That is something to see.'

I was suddenly stone-cold sober. My eyes were focusing, and his face, big enough in all conscience, was its normal size. 'South Sea pearls can be valuable,' I muttered, too relaxed.

'Ja, very valuable, that is true. Come below with me one moment Mr Ingram, I wish to show you something. It will take your breath away.'

He took my arm and steered me aft to the companionway. We went down the steps into the saloon and along a narrow passage from which cabins opened. The big one for'ard was his. It occupied most of the width of the vessel, one side tapering in with the slant of the bow, the other holding a door which led to his sleeping quarters and bathroom. I got a vague impression of cabinets and cupboards, a chart table and a dining table and chairs. It was hot down there after the open deck and I felt sweat start on my forehead, dampness on my palms.

He bent down in front of a large mahogany box that was bolted to both the side and the deck. He took a key from his pocket and turned it in the lock. I was leaning over his shoulder and I caught a glimpse of bare brown feet in gold sandals just behind me. He opened the cupboard and drew out a wooden tray covered by a piece of green baize. He put the tray on the chart table, drew back the baize.

'There,' he said, in little more than a whisper, 'look at this.' I saw a curiously-chased fine gold chain of apparent great antiquity. Each link was separated by a cluster of small rubies of a deep gleaming red. Between the rubies were huge pearls, twenty-five of them, differing considerably in shape, long rather than round, but all of an indescribable depth of colour. I was looking at the Balinese pearls.

11

I woke up with a garage man's oil-rag and the remains of last week's Scotch broth in my mouth. I had a head like a compressed bale of cotton and as many spots before my eyes as if I'd just done fifteen rounds with Mohammed Ali in his prime. I climbed out of bed as if I was carrying a power station on my back and diving boots on my feet. I staggered into the shower and sluiced myself under water as cold as I could get it. I dried off and stared at myself in the mirror. I looked like a million dollars in counterfeit notes all packed in the suitcases under my eyes.

I had to take long rests between getting the stubble off my chin and finding a clean shirt and some slacks. I rested again between each sock and shoe. This is tough, I said to myself, but you can lick it. I made it through the heat to the restaurant, screwing up my eyes against the sun. Black coffee. Lots and lots of black coffee.

I was on my third cup and beginning to celebrate my return to civilisation when she came. Jacky. She was in a blue and white polka-dot outfit with a matching neck scarf and looked as bright and fresh as I was broken-down and dejected. She swept into the dining room with full power going in both boilers and dropped her hook at my table.

'My God,' she cried, 'You look like the last of the Mohicans.'

'Good morning,' I replied politely, 'I've no idea what the last Mohican looked like but I am prepared to accept it as a compliment. Would you mind dropping your voice to a whisper, however? This a.m. finds me somewhat fragile.'

'I'd say. Boy, were you happy or were you happy?'

'I was happy.'

'Some escort. You slept on my shoulder all the way back to town.'

'It was a nice shoulder.'

'And you took just a little waking when we arrived here. I don't suppose you remember that?'

'It's all a little vague. I have to admit I

do not have too clear a recollection of how the party ended.'

'No kidding? Long before it ended you insulted one-half of the guests and ignored the other half. That was when you were not spooning in the moonlight.'

'Disgraceful.'

'And you gave Madame Zahl a real looking over.'

'Shocking. Though I appreciate a beautiful woman. I'm afraid I don't remember much of any of these things.'

'Before that you disappeared below with mine host. Were you sick?'

'Ah, now that I do remember and I must correct you. I went below at mine host's suggestion and I was not sick.'

'What kind of games went on down there? I noticed the fatal oriental went with you.'

'Nothing like that at all. Herr Zahl wished to show me something.'

I drank some more coffee and watched her from over my cup. That is not as easy as it sounds: it's a good way of getting coffee down your tie.

'Oh,' she said a little too calmly,

'something interesting?'

'Some people would think so.'

I could see her making up her mind to pursue the subject.

'Well? Don't be so cagey,' she prodded.

'Just old photographs.'

I had no reason for saying photographs. It was merely the first thing that came into my aching head. But it was something that Jacky found disconcerting. I saw a momentary flash of alarm in her eyes, a briefly frozen smile on her carmine lips.

She shrugged. 'Oh, photographs,' she said deprecatingly, but in a slightly strangled voice.

'Yes. That guy's been all over the world you know. Acapulco, Rio, Zanzibar, Tahiti — you name it, he's been there.'

'Yes, of course.' She glanced around the room while she recovered her poise. 'Aren't you going to buy me a drink? Or is coffee all you can stomach?'

'Forgive me, I'm not myself this morning.'

I shepherded her through into the bar and we took high stools and leaned our elbows on the counter. I ordered her a Tom Collins and a tomato juice for myself. She drew on the straw and looked at me speculatively from the corner of her eyes.

'Andrée has been getting at you, hasn't she?'

'Getting at me?'

'You know what I mean.'

'I'm not sure it is any of your business.'

'It isn't. I thought it was kind to warn you. She does it all the time, just for kicks. She loves to see the guys come running. It doesn't mean a damn thing.'

'To be fair, she told me as much. And I'm pretty durable.'

'That's good. Not everyone is. Some guys get the wrong idea and fall overboard.'

'I have my feet firmly planted on the deck.'

We sipped our drinks and thought our own private thoughts.

'Been getting anything interesting from Max?' she asked after a little while.

'Yes, he has come up with one little item. I'm looking into it.'

'Good old Max. I knew he would deliver.'

She finished her drink and stared at her watch. 'My goodness, I never dreamed it was so late. I'll have to fly. I have to get back and help.'

'Help?'

'Yes. That's what I came here to tell you and I almost forgot. Andrée has arranged the party, the one for the people on the list. This evening, at eight.'

'I'll be there.'

I walked her to the car. She had the key in the ignition and paused.

'Perhaps I should mention Andrée's parties go on rather late. I mean late: sometimes there's still the odd couple in the shrubbery at dawn. Think you can make it to the end?'

She didn't wait for an answer. She roared the engine suddenly and was gone in a cloud of dust. I went back to the restaurant, drank more coffee and toyed with a salad. Then I gave that up and went to my room and stretched out on the bed. I had to make my mind up about something. The next move. By chance I now knew where the pearls were. By sheer chance — or was it? What I didn't know was why they were there or how they got there. Or how I could get them back. One solution stared me in the face, but simply because it was so obvious I was not prepared to buy it. Carl had wanted money. He had taken the pearls and sold them to Zahl, though he would have to persuade Zahl that they were his to sell. Since Zahl had the pearls, that suggested Andrée was unaware where they had gone: she would hardly have risked taking me to his yacht, the very place where the pearls were.

The whole thing was too simple, too self-evident, and yet had too many improbabilities about it. Plausible and yet implausible. A false trail that was deliberately designed to mislead. But I couldn't see where the true trail even began. And my head ached too much to figure it out. I drew the curtains, set my travelling alarm for seven and took two paracetamols. In two minutes I was asleep. I dreamed of a beautiful damsel held to ransom by an evil pirate on his outlawed vessel and I was the swashbuckling hero who fought his cut-throat crew to a standstill. Against uncounted swords and muskets I slashed my way to the rascally captain's cabin. In his lair the damsel screamed with fear as a Sumatran tiger threatened to leap on her, while the pirate chief gloated in the background. He put the Balinese pearls round his neck, but they immobilised him and I raised my sword to cut him down. I woke up in a sweat and got up and showered. The captain looked like a maniacal Zahl, the damsel was Andrée — who else?

12

By the time I got there the party had got its second wind. The big sitting-room had been cleared for dancing and a number of couples swayed to the pop music of a record-player. A cold buffet table was on the terrace, and a little distance off was stationed a gamelan orchestra. The plaintive music of the island produced more atmospheric background for the people clustered at the buffet and those who strolled the paths of the garden. There were perhaps forty people altogether, and I remembered that Andrée's list had extended to some twenty names, so presumably she had all or most of them there.

Andrée introduced me to Charles Kindleberger, the tall dark, handsome and supposedly mysterious businessman. He didn't seem so mysterious to me. He was just back from his latest trip, cagey about his business maybe, but ready enough to talk on other matters. He had arrived only that afternoon from Sydney and we exchanged impressions about the big city, the splendour of the harbour and the dullness of the suburbs, the way that property had skyrocketed and how Paddington, the old run-down inner-city slum area, had come back up as a fashionable place to live, the old terrace houses there refurbished, the decorative ironwork, brought out originally as ballast in the sailing vessels, restored and trimly painted. We talked about the great opera house complex and the mistakes that had been made with it: especially the choice of the second hall as the opera house, so that they had spent a hundred million dollars on an opera house and still did not have an auditorium large enough to house grand opera. And Sutherland had complained of the acoustics!

He had seen her when he was there, in her great role in *Norma*. I dismissed him from the case: a true grand opera buff simply couldn't be involved in grand larceny.

Next I met Marina Maxwell, the lady

whose husband had gone missing. She was tall, lean and tense, a little like an emaciated Lauren Bacall (and she was slim enough). She talked with a somewhat abstracted air as if her mind were a long way off — somewhere in Borneo perhaps. She was drinking rather heavily and the more she drank the more abstracted she became. We chatted about Bali, the bad inflation and the problems that resulted. Her talk was erratic and perfunctory. But when the good Dr Schneider hove in sight, fresh from delivering his soothing homilies and unsoothing bills to his hotel patients, she became a lot more relaxed. I let her escape and noticed she was much more vivacious in his company. My hostess's suspicions were ill-founded: her husband was dead and she was casting her net for a replacement.

That left the elderly Dutch couple, the Van Hoorns. They were very polite, very affable, and at the same time they showed a certain reserve that formed a kind of barrier. I imagined they were sensitive of their status as reduced gentlefolk, poor relations at the feast, contrasting their own stretched resources, the well-kept but obviously well-worn clothes, with those around them. They had seen a great deal of change: they had once been the masters and now they were only here on sufferance. We talked about Jakarta when it was still Batavia, and the shock of the Japanese occupation. Those were times both to recall and to forget.

In between were many more. The beer-swilling Australian engineer who was something to do with the power station and talked exclusively of ohms, peak demand, load-shedding and the terrible strain imposed on him by the spread of air-conditioning. He had in tow a Balinese beauty in a tight-fitting sheath of a skirt that managed to be terrifically erotic by parting a little below the knee and showing a foot of brown legs. He was really 'into' Australian women, he told me in confidence, and tonight he was 'down-market'; I would not have said no to his bottom of the heap product.

There was a tennis enthusiast who had seen all the stars in action — Borg,

Connors, Nastase and the rest, and he gave me a tedious set by set account of endless great matches. What about the women, Billy-Jean King, Goolagong, et cetera? — pure pit-a-pat stuff, he sneered, a mere shadow of the real he-man game.

There was a young blonde who, as Mae West remarked, would rather be looked over than over-looked. She wore a gown that struggled to cover the bare essentials in front and waist-length, straight, straw-coloured hair that left her back to your imagination. Her face was meant to stop you in your tracks: deeply brown-shaded eyes that made you think she was made up for a part in a horror movie, long feathery earrings that must have tickled her neck, a slash of silvery-pink mouth, and a cute dimpled chin. It was a face that made you wonder what it looked like at eight a.m. She sloshed about a highball glass full of ice-cubes and gin, and she pushed her personality with a steam shovel. She was the kind of cutie who had the faded, already-married girls biting their fingernails and got their husbands more intimidated than interested.

I moved out to the terrace and away from the racket of the mechanical pop music. Half-hidden in velvet darkness the gamelan players struck their gongs and tapped their drums, faces dark, expressionless, impassive. The inscrutable East being inscrutable. I bumped — literally — into a slim, dark woman and fetched another drink to replace the spilled one. She had a face that came off no assembly line — widely set, mysterious eyes that smouldered, high cheekbones that suggested a touch of the orient, a sensuous mouth and firm chin. She had a deep, rich voice that went well with the face, the stylish black gown, and she talked a lot of sense with a lot of charm. I was just getting into my stride when her husband arrived: skinny, insignificant with horn-rimmed glasses and a nervous manner. There's no accounting for taste, but I could understand his nervousness, married to that fire-bomb.

And there was — there always is — the rotund, bald-headed middle-aged bachelor, the life and soul of the party. He stood by the bar and kept a posse of admirers amused with his tales and repartee. I heard the end of one story and its punch-line: 'No fella, I said 'I'm in the mood, not in the nude!''

A little after midnight I prospected the ruins of the buffet and collected a few bits of cold chicken, ham, tomatoes, and fresh oranges soaked in vodka. It was the first solid food I'd had in thirty-six hours and I needed it.

'I am sorry there is so little left. They seem a voracious crowd, do they not?' Andrée was standing in the shadows as I cleaned up my plate.

'I've had plenty. Can I get you something?'

'No, I've eaten.'

'Good party,' I grunted, 'just swell-elegant, as a Sinclair Lewis character would say.'

'I suppose that's a compliment of sorts,' she laughed. Then more soberly: 'I hope you met everyone — you know what I mean.'

'Yes, I did. Interesting bunch.'

'But tiresome after a while. Care to accompany me on a little stroll? I'll just fetch a wrap. I won't be a moment.'

She came back with a silk wrap round her shoulders that didn't look as if it would provide more protection than a cobweb. We walked along by the pool and over to the far side of the garden. There was a shadowed patch of grass, still and dark.

'I don't think any of these people had anything to do with the pearls,' I commented after a little while.

'So we are back to where we started.'

'No. One is never right back to the start. One has progressed, one understands a little more.'

'Do you have new ideas, Harry?'

'I think we have to look much nearer home.'

She lay back on the grass, the wrap falling from her shoulders and her eyes starry in the darkness. She lay like that a long time. Then she said: 'Kiss me.'

I turned on my side and looked down at her. All I could see clearly was the eyes.

'We went through this routine before, remember?'

'Don't be cruel,' she whispered, 'I need love.'

I kissed her once and lay very close to her. I got the sweet fragrance of her hair, her perfume. We lay there like that a long time, listening to the bushes tremble in the eddies of hot night air, the rustle of hidden night creatures against the strident chorus of grasshoppers.

'We had better go back,' I said after a long time.

'No need. Most people will have gone, and those who have not won't miss us.'

There was another long silence. Then she added: 'However, it would be more comfortable inside.'

We went back by the dark and silent pool, and past the place where the gamelan orchestra had sat. Men and instruments were gone. One solitary couple still danced to the record-player, the *risqué* blonde and a tall gangling lad with a crew cut. His arms were clasped round her back under her long hair.

I followed Andrée along the now familiar path that led to the garden entrance of her room. She switched on a bedside lamp, drew the curtains but left open one of the doors beyond. She threw off her wrap, kicked off her shoes, studied her face in the mirror for a long moment and went to the cabinet that held the bottles.

'Drinks?' she asked.

'No thanks, I've had enough.'

'Coffee? I can ring for some to be made.'

'It's half-past one. The servants won't thank you for making coffee at this hour.'

'Oh, they won't care. The clock doesn't exist in this house.'

'I decline to aid and abet you.'

'Then that only leaves me. All I have left to offer.' She threw herself back on the bed, arms stretched out, gown half up her legs. I sat on the bed beside her.

'This is just for kicks, isn't it?' I croaked. It was more of a comment than a question.

She stared up at me, head and shoulders framed by the soft blue of the coverlet. 'Yes and no,' she said slowly. 'Yes, it is a kick because I enjoy a handsome man just as you enjoy a beautiful woman. And no, because it's more than just a new conquest. I really do

132

love you, Harry. We could be good together.'

'I am a lot older than you. And what about Carl?'

'Age doesn't come into it. I like experienced men, so much more mature. Carl, he's strong and brave and he's worked for months in the jungle, living rough in a tent, with tigers prowling round at night and days spent in wading streams and ploughing through swamps, burning off the leeches with a cigarette — that takes guts. Not many men would want it, I guess. At the same time he's just a baby, a big, beautiful, muscular baby who loves to be admired — if only by middle-aged deprived female tourists who've never before been west of Seattle or south of Tijuana. Why he wouldn't come this evening — it's gala night at the Bali International, you see, and he can't miss that. I guess he doesn't know what he really does want.'

'He wants money.'

She opened her eyes wide and stared at me. She relaxed again. One sinuous arm cradled my neck. 'Kiss me, Harry,' she whispered.

I put my arms around her and kissed her. I kissed her a long time and then I took my lips away, about one inch away.

'That's why you gave him the pearls,' I whispered.

I felt a slight tremble of the shoulders, an intake of breath. Or did I imagine these things? I have a powerful imagination.

'It was set up that way,' I continued. 'You began to keep the pearls in the Japanese box only weeks before they disappeared, and you made sure everybody knew about it, by appearing to shoot your mouth off at one of your parties. So they could seem to be stolen without the safe being cracked.'

Her face was all sweet innocence but the voice was cold. 'Why would I do that?'

'So Carl can make himself rich, get his gold out of Sumatra.'

She sat up on one elbow, alert, earnest. 'If you think that then you don't know Carl. He wouldn't take anything from me, not money, not pearls, not just for that. He would rather leave the gold where it is, deep in the jungle.'

'Deep in the jungle. You know, I wonder about this find of his, I really do. It comes too pat, too convenient, he's too willing to talk about it, and it can't be checked on.'

'Why should he invent it?'

'I don't know, yet. To cover something else, something that really has to be kept under wraps. One thing I'm sure of — the pearls are not the object of all this, they are only the link.'

She lay down again and sighed. 'I don't know what you're talking about. All I know is the pearls are gone and you are supposed to be finding them for me. And while you're doing that one little thing you could treat me nice. Kiss me again.'

I kissed her hard and long and held my face touching hers.

'I've given up looking for the pearls,' I said. There was a long silence.

'Oh, why?'

I thought I could detect tension in the whisper in my ear. Perhaps it was only my own tension: I had a beautiful woman in my arms.

'Because I know where they are.'

She stretched away from me. Her eyes were really wide open now.

'They are in a cupboard on a big yacht, and that yacht is over the mountains in Singaradja. The yacht of Hermann Zahl. I saw them there last night.'

13

She continued to stare wide-eyed. I got up and went round to the cabinet.

'I'll have that drink now,' I growled, 'may I pour you one?'

'There's no ice again,' she said calmly enough, sitting up and turning towards me. 'Scotch please. That goes down best without ice.'

I poured out two stiff jolts of the Bell's and took hers round to her.

'You're not kidding me?' she asked, 'you really did see the pearls?'

'Yes, really. Zahl has them locked in a box down below in his cabin. They looked genuine enough, but you could tell for sure.'

'How did they get there, Harry?'

'I was hoping you might be able to tell me that. It might have been a straight deal between him and whoever took them. He was unlikely to know about their being kept in the open box, so someone took them and sold them to him, perhaps through an intermediary.'

She sat now with her knees drawn up to her chin, one hand holding the Scotch, the other curled round her legs. 'Why did he show them to you, Harry?'

'Just possibly it was sheer luck — he was talking about pearl fishing. More likely, he knows I am looking for them and he is after making a deal.'

'He wants to sell them back?'

'That would be my idea. He didn't say so. He would certainly know you have a lot of money. He might even know your money is tied up, but that I might be able to get the insurance company to play ball.'

She walked to the dressing table, put down her glass and casually did things to her hair. 'Is that what you propose to do, Harry?'

'I was hoping to establish one or two little preliminaries first,' I grunted, 'that the pearls really were stolen, in the first place. You say you did not give them to Carl to finance his Sumatra project, and presumably you did not give them to anyone else.'

'That is correct.' She ran over to me and threw both arms round my neck. 'Don't you believe me?'

Sweet, beautiful innocence again. I kissed her and held her tight. 'Do you kiss all your clients so nicely?' she asked coquettishly, 'the young female ones, I mean.'

'I get very few young female clients, even fewer who are beautiful, and none who care to discuss the case in the bedroom.'

'I'm so glad.'

I carried her over to the bed and turned off the light. I held her while the curtains shivered in the night breeze and the scent-laden air wafted us into oblivion.

I'm not sure whether it was her first stirring or the subdued morning light that woke me. I felt, rather than saw, her leave the bed and I heard the thrumming of the shower. She was back in the white robe, her face fresh and bright.

'Let's go, Harry,' she cried cheerfully, 'let's go to Singaradja and get the pearls.'

I looked at my watch. Not even seven. 'Plenty of time,' I said inconsequentially.

'No,' urgently, 'I want to go. Now. I want to have the pearls back.'

I got up and showered and put on last evening's clothes. She'd had a breakfast tray brought to the room while I was in the bathroom. We drank coffee and ate crisp fresh rolls in silence. There was a suppressed excitement about her face, her movements. I thought then it was the prospect of recovering the pearls. Later I had other ideas.

We walked briskly over to the yard where the Mercedes stood and headed out for Singaradja. She drove very fast with silent concentration and that same suppressed energy. At that hour there was plenty of people and bicycles on the road, but little other traffic. We ripped through the busier streets of Denpasar, roared past the still serenity of Mengwi and hit seventy on the long, straight, narrow slope up to Lake Beratan. We flew over the pass and the tyres screamed on the bends going down into Singaradja. The little port lay peaceful and unhurried, like the remote outpost it had become. Then there was the jetty, now with fewer vessels — the little fishing boats were missing.

She strode athletically along the uneven planks, long slender legs bare beneath the plain silk dress. I followed her up the elaborate gangway. Once on deck she stopped suddenly as if uncertain what to do next.

Her look told me she, too, had noticed the silence. An empty ship is like an uninhabited house; you know it is empty the moment you cross the threshold.

I walked quickly for'ard. No one on the deck or the bridge. My watch read a little after nine. We had made it very fast. Nine was a time when somebody should be cleaning ship, doing a little painting or putting in some work on the engine. There was nobody.

I called out three times but all I did was scare the seabirds into wheeling noisily overhead. Andrée followed me down the companionway and along the passage. The door to Zahl's cabin stood open. I went through and looked at the cupboards and cabinets, the open bathroom door and last at the chart table. Andrée pressed behind me in the doorway and I held her back with one arm. He was there by the chart table, lying face down, with a patch of blood oozing from under his pyjama jacket. There was a bright red cut and a livid bruise on the side of his head where he had fallen against the chart table. But that hadn't killed him. I turned him over. The pay-off was the bullet wound in the chest, just below the heart. The jacket was seared round the hole, meaning he had been shot at point-blank range.

One arm stretched out straight from his shoulder. It pointed to the heavy box bolted to the deckhead, three feet from where he lay. It was as if he was groping for the pearls. But the door of the box stood open, the key still in the lock, and the pearls were gone.

14

There were over a hundred people in the big courtyard of the old royal palace in Denpasar. It was difficult to see if Vetran was in the crowd because my seat was right at the front by the stage where all the light was concentrated. I craned my head, but beyond the first two or three rows were only indistinct shapes and shadows. Even the gamelan orchestra was shrouded in darkness, excepting only the two drummers who squatted cross-legged on the stage itself.

It was the Legong dance and the performance began before I could find Vetran. The four young girls who open the ballet were on the stage, scattering petals and performing the precise stilted movements of body and legs, the positioning of the arms and posturing of the fingers, and the sudden sideways movement of the eyes — all of which required great physical control and years of training. They were followed by the senior dancers who played the major parts in the story, a love story, although the male role too was played by a woman. They had an evident superiority of technique, of presence. No very fast movement, no leaping or pirouetting, not a lot of movement at all, yet there was fascination in the slight changes in the position of hands and fingers, the movement of the eyes in expressionless, immobile faces. I was near enough to see all the detail of the gorgeous costumes in green, red and gold, and to see the perspiration course down the girls' foreheads. I was too near: the perspiration made them human, spoiled the illusion of supernatural self-possession and effortless grace.

Vetran was waiting for me, trailing behind the rest of the audience. He was at the entrance, standing by a car, and he asked me politely to get in. He gave directions to the driver in his own language and in a low tone.

'I hope you enjoyed the performance, Mr Ingram,' he said in his near-perfect

English. 'The royal company have the best Legong you can see in the whole of Bali.'

'It was excellent. I couldn't find you there. I thought perhaps you had seen so many performances you decided to skip it.'

'Oh, no, certainly not. I was a little late and I squeezed into the back. No, you can never see enough Legongs. It is the same thing as classical concerts in Europe or performances of familiar operas. Every performance is different, and in its difference memorable.'

'You have been in Europe much?'

'Yes, and in America. But, as you say in Britain, there is no place like home, and to me Bali is home. Indeed, it is to my home we are going now. Not very far from the town. I think we can discuss business there more pleasantly than in my office.'

We were already out of Denpasar, moving north west, I guessed, and the air was fresher and cooler and without the characteristic odours of the streets. I was curious about this meeting: Vetran had suggested we meet at the Legong dance. At the time it seemed a little odd; now it appeared a form of wily oriental thinking, a device for putting me in the right frame of mind — for what?

The car turned in at a driveway and in the headlights I got a glimpse of an old-fashioned bungalow, neither large nor small, an extent of grounds, somewhat overgrown. An elderly female servant stood in the porch and bowed us indoors. There was a large square room, very inadequately lit, so that all the light was in the centre and the corners remained vague and remote. It reminded me of the palace courtyard we had just left. There were large comfortable chairs round a low table: I could distinguish little else. Vetran spoke quickly to the servant.

'We shall have some wine, Mr Ingram. It is a white, a Pouilly fuissé, one of the best of the French whites, I think. I have it specially imported. I hope you will like it.'

'I'm sure it is exactly what a hot night like this calls for.'

It was not only the night that was hot.

The room seemed to have retained all the accumulated heat that the sun had poured on it during the day. The warm air filtering through the windows was tired and damp, as if from the open door of a laundry. I felt the sweat start on my forehead and round my neck, the beads of salty moisture trickle down my chest and back, the shirt and lightweight slacks sticking to my body. It must have been over a hundred in there.

Vetran opened the wine with practised ease and poured it into two elegantly slim glasses. A perfect white, well chilled, but not so much as to kill its dry, full flavour. The refrigerated liquid made me sweat all the more. I mopped my neck and forehead with a handkerchief. Vetran seemed as cool as the proverbial cucumber. Asiatics must have their body thermostat set higher.

It was very quiet in there. A heavy growth of trees and shrubs masked the house from the road. Occasionally I glimpsed the momentary beams of headlights but there was practically no sound. The house itself was silent as the grave. A little time, silent, superheated time, drifted by.

'I predicted you would come to me in a few days,' Vetran volunteered at last, with a smile. 'I presume you have not yet been able to solve the mystery of the pearls, Mr Ingram.'

'Let's say I'm simply curious to know what it is you have to sell. I suppose it is something that has a price, and therefore it is valuable.'

'Oh, yes, indeed, very valuable. To the right person.'

'Well?'

'I should explain, Mr Ingram, that what I have to show you is not direct evidence concerning the disappearance of the pearls. But I am quite sure it is closely connected with that matter.'

'What are you asking for it?'

He leaned forward to pour more wine, then came upright and smiled at me.

'Ten per cent. The pearls, I believe, are conservatively valued at one million dollars, so ten per cent will be one hundred thousand.'

I whistled. 'In my league that's an awful

lot of bread. This has got to be something fantastic.'

'Not so much fantastic, Mr Ingram, as dangerous — to the party concerned. You would like to see what it is that can be worth so much?'

I sipped the wine and nodded at him. He left the room and I heard vague sounds in the distance that might have been a safe door being opened and a drawer slid out. He returned with an envelope in his hand. He put the envelope on the table under the light and took from it six postcard-sized photographs. He spread the photographs in a row in front of me. They were not first-class shots but good enough for the purpose. Evidently taken by flash, with the unreal light that gives a picture. The subjects were perfectly clear. The first showed a section of a row of buildings, only one building in fact, with small parts of those on either side. The building had a bricked-in window on the ground floor and a solid door at the side, badly in need of paint. The sign on the door could be easily read: 'The Amneris Club. Private.

Members Only'. The next shot was of an interior. It showed people sitting at tables and chairs and beyond them a low stage, brightly lit. The club-room itself, it was logical to suppose. The third, fourth, fifth and sixth photographs showed the same stage with a girl on it. She took a different pose in each shot, the sort of pose that X-films and girlie magazines have made familiar. The girl was a brunette, tall, slim and attractive, and she was completely nude. The last two shots showed her face and body very close. There was a wild look about her face, a glazed appearance about the eyes, a slackness of the mouth. I knew both the face and the body. I knew them very well. Andrée.

Vetran collected up the six prints and replaced them in the envelope. He took his glass and sipped, standing a little back in the shadows beyond the circle of light. I tapped on the table with my left hand, meaninglessly.

'I suppose that is the whole collection and you have the negatives?' I growled, suppressing the tension, forgetting for a moment the beads of moisture running down my back.

'The answer to both of those questions is yes.'

'And I suppose you have no intention of telling me how they came into your possession?'

'Again the answer is yes.'

'What makes you think they are worth a hundred thousand?'

'The lady would not want them sold to an American scandal sheet, I presume.'

'Probably not. But it is just possible she wouldn't care.'

'Then there is the connection with the pearls.'

'What connection? I see nothing in the photographs that connects.'

'You disappoint me, Mr Ingram. I thought that with your reputation you would see the connection immediately. The pearls were taken to pay for the photographs. A little case of blackmail. It is very simple.'

'Not from where I sit,' I grunted. 'The deal never went through. The pictures are still here and you don't have the pearls. At least you didn't have them forty-eight hours ago.'

He laughed and paused to refill the glasses again. 'No, that is quite true, I do not have the pearls. Someone else has them, perhaps the person who also has the original negatives and prints of these pictures. You see, Mr Ingram, these are merely copies.'

'And you expect to get a hundred thousand for copies?'

'Yes. For these and something else. A name.'

'The name of the owner of the originals?'

'Not quite. It is the name of a person who knows the identity of the owner of the originals. From the name I can give you it should be perfectly easy to get back to the owner.'

I thought about it while I sipped more wine. It had a sour taste now. I was aware again of the perspiration now running down my legs as well as everywhere else. That room was as hot as a Hong Kong brothel in August. Or perhaps it was those pictures that had me sweating.

'I'll have to check back,' I said at last. 'It may turn out you have nothing to sell, that what you know is already known by someone else.'

Vetran shrugged his shoulders and smiled. 'Then you save your client a lot of money. We shall see.'

'Yes, we shall see. Thanks for the wine.' I got up and headed towards the dim outline of the door. 'Oh, in case you were wondering, I prefer the Balinese style of eroticism. The Legong is so much more clever and civilised.'

'You reveal much discrimination, Mr Ingram.'

The car was waiting for me in the driveway. After that room even the sticky plastic of the car seats, the warm chrome of the fittings, seemed icy to the touch. The same driver took me back to town, without a word.

15

It was an hour later. I had showered and changed out of my sweat-sodden clothes. And I was standing again by my old buddies, the two stone figures with the idiotic smiles. Perhaps I was beginning to look like them myself.

Jacky slid open the door and let me into the hall. 'It's rather late,' she grumbled, 'I know you said it was urgent, but do you realise what time it is?'

I gave her my friendly grin. 'Your boss informs me the clock doesn't exist in this establishment. I have to talk to you. Something has come up.'

'Everyone has gone to bed,' she said.

'But you were still up, reading. You have your glasses on.'

She flushed and snatched them off. 'You had better come along to my room,' she said haughtily, 'you can say what you have to say there, undisturbed.'

I followed her along a covered walkway

to one of the separate blocks of rooms. Her bedroom, I guessed, stood opposite that of Andrée, but completely screened from it by the space of the pool, lawns and several dense clumps of shrubs. It was a harder, less feminine room, the hangings and bed-linens in a matching modern design in brown and white, not the soft pastel blues of the bedroom I already knew. The French windows were open to the night air and we sat on the verandah with no light to attract the bugs. It was still a hot night. Out on the verandah it was probably over eighty, but that was twenty degrees lower than the sweatpot I had come from.

'You said something had come up.'

I spoke slowly, choosing my words. 'Yes. When you came to the hotel yesterday we spoke about the party on Zahl's yacht.'

I expected her to burst in to tell me Zahl was dead. But she didn't. Perhaps that news had not got to her yet.

'Yes, I remember.'

'I told you he took me to his cabin to see some photographs.' I tried to observe her reactions but in the dark it was difficult to see her face at all.

'I don't really recall any detail. I think you did say something about photographs.'

'I thought you would remember that. I got the impression it interested you.'

'No. Why should it?'

'Because now I've seen some other photographs.'

She didn't respond. I would have given a lot to see her face.

'Photographs of Andrée. I wonder if you know the ones I mean.'

She still didn't say anything.

'All right, I'll spell it out. These are not happy holiday snaps. These are pictures that most girls wouldn't want taken, let alone passed around, and certainly not published.'

'Where did you see them?'

'That's beside the point at the moment. What I am asking is what do *you* know about them?'

There was a long pause. 'I know what they are. Andrée performing in her birthday suit.'

'Tell me what else you know.'

'It was four years ago, just after the air crash that killed her parents. She was nineteen.' She sounded very relaxed but her voice was without inflexion, deliberately so. Jacky too was choosing her words now. 'She went through a wild period, did some crazy things. Maybe it was the crash. Maybe she just has a wild streak in her — I think that sometimes.'

'Go on.'

'Well, she was into drugs, drink, wild parties. Sometimes she went off on a wingding and wouldn't show up for days. At first it seemed like teenage nonsense, just a phase lots of kids go through, and she'd come out of it. But it got worse. She got to hanging around dives, got in with a way-out bunch, people who went to private clubs. The sort of clubs where you can see certain kinds of shows . . . way-out shows, you know what I mean. Sex performances would be the correct term.'

'Like the Amneris Club?'

'Yes.' Her voice rose in surprise. 'That and others.'

'Where was this?'

'In LA. She saw the professional strippers do their stuff and reckoned she could give a better show, I guess. Of course she was tanked up on hash or alcohol, or maybe both.'

'Who took the photographs?'

'Who knows? Those clubs have a no cameras rule, but it's not easy to enforce. It would be very simple to conceal one of those tiny cameras they have now and use a really fast film. Or even use flash. With those psychedelic lights flashing incessantly who is going to notice a camera flash or two? Especially when all eyes are riveted on the stage.'

'It was a mixed audience, men and women?'

'Sure. There had to be a club member in the party but that could be easily fixed. Businessmen took their friends, guys took their girls. They'd all be high.'

'You went yourself?'

'Once or twice. I went with the chauffeur we had in those days. I bought a membership so I could keep an eye on her, see if we could persuade her to come home nights. Not many women would care for a show like that, not unless they were a little kinky themselves.'

'You were not there when the photographs were taken?'

'No. And she didn't perform when I was there.'

'She performed on the spur of the moment? It wasn't arranged?'

'That's right.'

'Then whoever had the camera handy either had a lucky break or knew in advance she was likely to do something like that?'

'I guess so. But some guys might have a camera there all the time, just hoping for the unusual to happen.'

'But he would have to know she was somebody, an heiress?'

'Say, what is this, third degree? All you need are the bright lights, the rubber cosh.'

'I'm sorry. I'm trying to get the full picture. Just give me a few more minutes.'

She got up abruptly and went into the bedroom. A light was switched on. I heard the clink of glass, the gurgling of liquid emerging from a bottle's mouth.

She came back with two glasses, put one in my hand.

'Not what you specified,' she murmured. 'I don't have the Beaune '77, the Glenfiddich or the Courvoisier. Just plain Bourbon. Bourbon or nothing.'

I tasted it. 'But swell Bourbon.'

'The rest of the specification I can provide. That's swell too.'

'I wouldn't doubt it. Just let me get a few more answers. How did you get to know about the photographs?'

'The photographs. We're back to those. You have a one-track mind.'

'They do seem to be important.'

She paused and put down her glass. 'It was five or six months back, soon after we arrived out here. Andrée got a letter. It enclosed one of the prints, mentioned others, and asked for a quarter of a million dollars.'

'You saw the letter?'

'She showed it to me. It worried her. Up to that time she had no idea any photos existed. And meanwhile she'd taken the cure, kicked the drugs and got out of that scene.'

I consumed Bourbon while I cogitated. Powerful medicine for cogitation, ninety-six proof. 'Let me see if I've got this straight. The photographs were taken about four years ago?'

'Right.'

'But whoever took them did nothing with them for over three years — until about six months ago, in fact. He waited all that time to put the bite on her.'

'That's right. But don't you see? He couldn't be sure the bite would take until she'd turned respectable and meant to stay so. Perhaps he waited in the expectation she would marry. That would have increased the pressure.'

'Yes, I see that. But — ' I decided against saying what I had on the tip of my tongue. Instead I said something else: 'But what happened then?'

'Nothing happened. We talked it over and she decided to call the bluff.'

She got up impatiently and I followed her into the room. She drew the curtains behind me and then went over by the bed, the one light burning behind her so that her face was in shadow.

'She heard no more about it?' I asked.

'Not so far as I am aware. But then . . . when the pearls were gone I . . . I wondered about a connection.'

'You thought the pearls went to buy the photographs?'

'It seems a possibility.'

'But it can't be that way. Somebody still has the photographs.'

'That's what I don't understand,' she said impatiently. 'Who has them? And who has the pearls?'

'I wish I knew.'

'But you have seen the photographs?'

'Yes.'

'I don't understand that either. Somebody's nuts around here and it isn't me.'

She put her arms around my shoulders and pressed her firm lithe body against me. I held her and kissed her. I kissed her as the Bourbon burned my brain, the scent of her body intoxicated my senses. She took one arm away and began to unbutton her blouse. It was one of those awkward models that has a myriad of tiny buttons all the way down the back.

'You could help,' she said softly, 'it

would speed things up.'

I put a hand on hers that was half-way down the buttons.

'We got as far as this before.'

'You said then the conditions weren't right, remember?'

'I'm not sure they are now. I don't think we quite trust one another. That is not a good basis for love.'

I still had my hand on hers. My fingers felt the softness of the skin under the blouse, the warmth of her flesh.

'The trust seems all to be on one side,' she spat, suddenly frigid. 'I've told you all I know. You've told me nothing.'

'What is it you want to know?'

'Who showed you the photographs of Andrée?'

'I can't tell you that. Professional reasons and all that jazz, you understand.'

She pulled away from me suddenly, marched over to the windows and pulled the curtains back half-way. The moon was bright now and the garden was coldly clear in its pale light. 'I think we lost the mood,' she cried harshly. 'I'll take a raincheck, give it a whirl some better evening, when you have no secrets to keep.'

'Yes, let's wait for a better evening.'

I went through the French windows and down the steps of the verandah into the garden. This was the screwiest case I was ever on. The women were giving it me with both barrels and I didn't have a chance. There was a catch in it somewhere, there had to be. But perhaps I shouldn't work too hard at finding it.

16

My guess was right. Jacky's room was opposite the pool, on the other side of it from Andrée's room. I went by bushes and flower beds and a little lawn and there it was, the water dark and fathomless in the moonlight. In the pool something moved faintly, or rather water rippled against something that lay motionless just breaking the surface. I crept to the edge and knelt down on the paving trying to get a closer view. Now I could get an idea of its dimensions. Just about the size of a body, an adult body.

I slipped off my slacks and shirt and peeled off shoes and socks. I plunged from the side and broke surface a yard away from the body. The shock waves from my plunge surged around it and suddenly it began to move very fast across the water. A corpse that could swim. I went after it, caught it up, grasped a shoulder, a slim smooth arm. I had her pinned against the side of the pool and she held on to the rail by the other arm.

'I thought you'd drowned, you little idiot,' I gasped.

She laughed and pulled the wet hair from her face. 'It's so hot, tonight, I couldn't sleep. Do you enjoy moonlight bathing, Harry?'

She suddenly plunged away out of reach. I swam after her and there we were together out of breath on the other side of the pool. 'How did you guess . . . I would happen along?' I gasped.

'I had no idea . . . I often take a swim in the middle of the night when it's hot and I can't sleep.'

She darted away again, twisting and turning like a fish, up and down the pool. Again I went after her and at last she came to a stop near the shallow end where the water was waist-deep. She stood there, panting, her head thrown back, quite naked. I came up to her and she leaned back against me, panting, laughing and panting again.

'I'm faster than you, Harry . . . much

faster . . . You'd never catch me unless I let you.'

I drew hair away from her lips and kissed her. She crumpled up against me and I held her, her whole body trembling fast and breathing fast against mine.

'Carry me out,' she demanded.

I waited another few seconds to get more breath. I had one arm round her shoulders and I put the other under her legs. I carried her like that to the three wide stone steps that led up out of the pool. I carried her up those and stood holding her on the paved surround. She put one hand over my wrist, the one that held her shoulder.

'Why, you still have on your wrist-watch, Harry.'

'Certainly. I've always wanted to see if it's as waterproof as the makers claim.'

'You can put me down now if you're tired.'

'No, I'm all right. That heavy breathing is natural. I'm not tired. I've been to the Legong dance, I've been entertained by a gentleman to white wine — Pouilly fuissé, no less — and I've been entertained by a lady to Bourbon, and I've just had a swim. What's next?'

'Carry me to bed.'

I carried her along the path and up the verandah steps to her room. I stood her upright in the middle of the floor and fetched a big bath sheet from the bathroom. I dried her hair and rubbed down her body. Then I carried her over to the bed and deposited her gently in the half-open side where she had lain, and drew up over her the pale blue sheet and coverlet that constituted the covers. I took the bath sheet back into the bathroom and showered. When I came back she had thrown back the covers again. She lay there with a mysterious half-smile on her lips and a question-mark in her eyes, and nothing on her body. I looked down on her for one long, long moment before I turned off the light.

It was still not completely dark. The moonlight etched into sharp relief the scatter of objects in its path, the straight edge of the curtain, the flatness of the mirror on the dressing table, the bristles of a hairbrush, the elegant line of a tall

Chinese vase, the squat shape of a Japanese trinket box that once held some pearls. She lay against me, both soft and fragile and hard and cool. The garden beyond the open windows was a thousand miles away, the pulsating squalor of Denpasar a million further off.

Afterwards she lay still a long time and I listened to her quiet, regular breathing, but I knew she hadn't slept. My own tiredness was past and I felt alert, restless. A hundred ideas chased around in my brain and only some of them had to do with the beautiful body that lay in my arms.

She nestled closer to me and sighed. 'Talk to me, Harry. Tell me you love me.'

'I love you.'

'Talk some more. I'm not sleepy.'

'I don't think you'll like what I want to talk about.'

'Try me.'

'Photographs. You know the ones I mean.'

I didn't detect any change in her voice, any slight tension in her body.

'Oh, those. I'd forgotten about them.'

'Like hell, you had. Somebody's sticking you up for a quarter of a million and that's something you don't forget in a hurry.'

She pulled away so that she could turn and see my face. 'Who told you that?'

'Jacky. A little earlier this evening. After I'd told her I knew about them.'

'I see. And how did you come to know about them?'

'That's something I didn't tell Jacky. I have my reasons for that. They may be quite wrong, but at the moment I don't want to tell her anything I don't have to. And it would help if you did the same.'

'All right. But you'll tell me?'

'Of course. You are the client. I have no right to keep anything from you.'

She pressed her face close to mine and I kissed her gently on the point of the cheekbone. Then, almost in a whisper: 'I asked you if you knew a Peter Vetran, remember? I was at his house tonight. He had copies there and he showed them to me. They are not the originals. He claims he doesn't know who has those, but he

170

does know someone who could lead me to the originals.'

'Did he tell you who that someone is?'

'No. He wants a hundred thousand dollars for the information and that seemed a little steep.'

She lay silent for a long minute.

'I wondered if you had any idea who it might be,' I went on. 'I don't want to get too far into Vetran's hands if we can play it some other way.'

She was still silent. I stopped whispering and spoke positively, firmly: 'You've got to level with me. I could do a much better job for you if I have all the information, not just what you choose to tell me. I can't work in the dark.'

'I thought you were looking for the pearls,' she breathed at last.

'You mean there is no connection?'

'That is precisely what I mean.'

'You're telling me the blackmail and the pearls are absolutely coincidental? You didn't give the pearls to somebody in order to get the photographs, and the deal came unstuck?'

'Don't you believe me?'

I didn't believe her. I couldn't believe her. I looked in the lovely eyes, the beautiful face that held only innocence and sincerity.

'I wish you would stick to the pearls,' she rasped. 'The photographs are none of your business.'

I got from under the sheet and sat on the bed. The moonlight had gone now but it was not yet dawn. The garden lay black and indistinguishable.

'You don't care if you never get the photographs?'

'At last you're getting the idea.'

'You wouldn't be ashamed if some scandal sheet plastered them all over the West Coast?'

'It wouldn't be the end of the world. That was then and this is now. A lot of people know the way I was and they are not people I care anything about.'

'But it could hurt someone you do care about.'

'If he really cared for me, it wouldn't trouble him.'

'Ah. And you think your people, if they were still here, would not be troubled either?'

She didn't reply to that one. It was too shrewd a blow, a little under the belt even. I went over to the open windows and felt the fresher outside air cool on my body.

'Harry,' she said more softly, 'You knew about the photographs when you made love to me tonight.'

'Yes, of course.'

'And yet, having seen them, you were not disgusted with me?'

'No. You've just said it. That was then and this is now.'

I went out and down into the garden to the pool. I found my clothes and put them on. I made my way out of the garden and on to the road. I walked a couple of miles before I found a taxi, stopped by a wayside Coca Cola stand. The morning light was clean and bright when I reached the hotel. I went to my room and showered. I stayed under the cooling water a long time, I had to wash all that woman scent off me. I'd had my fill of her, of both of them. I was up to my eyebrows with them. I pulled the curtains to keep out the sun and I went to bed.

17

The taxi dropped me outside the Hotel Lavinia and I went in through the hallway with the cracked, uneven tiles. The same three men still gambled at the same table. They looked as if they hadn't moved since I was there with Jacky four evenings before. A lot had happened since then.

There was no big woman at the stove this evening. I made my way unannounced across the broken ground to the rooms and the same dog growled and the same chickens flapped in protest. I remembered the right door from before and knocked. No reply. I knocked more loudly. A voice, Max's voice, a little muffled, said to come in.

He lay on the old iron bedstead with the torn mosquito net drooping overhead. The same gimcrack furniture stood in place, the same bookcase, the incongruous steel and plastic stand which held the record-player. Nothing had changed.

'Why, hello,' Max grunted, getting up a little cumbrously to sit on the bed. 'Why, I was just thinking I should be in touch with you, fella.'

There was a day's growth of stubble on his chin and his slacks and T-shirt were creased and soiled. He groped underneath and produced a bottle, the great-grandson, probably, of the one he produced before. 'Have a drink,' he urged huskily, 'everything goes better with a drink.' He ambled over to the shelf, rinsed two glasses in the washbasin and poured out two stiff drinks, exactly as the last time.

I sat with mine and nodded in appreciation of the Scotch.

'I wondered if you had anything new for me.'

'No, I don't think so. I'm looking into one or two leads, but nothing solid so far.'

We sat and eyed one another. Max stroked the black stubble on his chin. His skin was drawn, his eyes more sunken than when I saw him last. He looked as if he had been emptying quite a few bottles.

'There was a little excitement over at

Singaradja,' I said casually.

'Oh yes, what was that?'

'A man was shot dead, a man called Zahl. He owned a big yacht, must have had plenty of money. Didn't you hear about it?'

'No. We don't get to hear much about what goes on over the mountains.'

'I thought you would have heard about this one. You knew Zahl once, didn't you, when you were on the West Coast?'

It was a purely random shot in the dark, but it hit some kind of target.

'Yes, that's right. I knew him, now you mention it. Not well, you know. Just enough to say 'Hi' and perhaps sit with him at a bar once in a while.'

I had him at a disadvantage now I had scored. But I had to be careful: it would be so easy for him to see through my guesswork.

'I heard Zahl had some interests in Las Vegas about that time,' I said vaguely. 'I wondered if someone from those days caught up with him, someone with a grudge, an old score to settle.'

I tried to sound only half-interested,

just passing a dead hour in futile conversation. Max was casual too. That was on the surface. He might have been a shade slow in his replies but the whisky hadn't addled his brain.

'It's possible, I suppose,' he grunted, stifling a yawn, 'but not very likely. He covered his tracks pretty carefully. In his rackets you have to.'

'I heard he specialised in private clubs, the kind that provide the sort of entertainment you can't get at the Sands or the Tropicana.'

'I guess that's so. The seamier side of Vegas. Not that the gambling isn't seamy enough, the way it crazes people, makes them stand hour after hour just pulling a lever. But relatively respectable. He opened a call-girl business, also. That's legal in Nevada, you know, just like the gambling.'

'He had similar clubs in LA, I imagine.'

'I never heard of those,' Max muttered quietly. 'It's possible. It would be logical. Vegas is only a longish drive away. You could run them in tandem easily enough.'

'What were you doing yourself in those days, Max?'

He rose to top up the glasses, paused to study his face in the chipped mirror above the washbasin. 'I could sure do with a clean up,' he growled. He sat down and picked up his glass again. 'What was that again? Oh, yes, what I did in LA.'

He drank more whisky. 'Nothing much. I got around, drifted, I guess you'd say. Never kept any job very long. One time, though, I had my own security outfit, patrolling shops, guarding bank transfers and the like. It folded after a while. There were two little problems I never could lick — how to find good reliable guys who weren't just as likely to take off with the bank-roll, and how to pay for the armoured vans: they come expensive.'

He paused and swallowed reflectively. 'After that I was with an enquiry agency for a while. That was too much standing in the rain watching folks' bedroom windows, softening up hotel help, and helping them remember things they didn't really remember. Divorce business, you know, pretty unsavoury. After that I peddled pump equipment round the gas stations. Even drove hot cars once.'

'You seem to have been a lot around cars. Ever try a chauffeur's job?'

He glanced at me a little oddly at that. 'No, I never did. Lots of rich folk have chauffeurs in LA, and the job's a cinch, easy pickin's. But it never appealed to me. If I was going to drive a sweet new Cadillac I wanted it to be my own.'

'How did you come to meet Zahl?'

He waited a little before he answered that one. 'I don't really recall. I sort of knew him from ways back. Perhaps we handled his cash when I had the security business. Yes, that was probably it.'

'Seen much of him since you've been out here?'

'Nope. Never clapped eyes on him. I heard he brought his boat into Singaradja quite a bit.'

'He married a Balinese.'

'Yes, I heard that.' He contemplated the half-inch of whisky still in his glass. 'Woman called Kalika, I'm told. A village woman. God only knows how he met her.' He seemed lost in thought. 'Some of these women are darned attractive,' he said, almost to himself, 'and I don't mean

179

just the young girls. The mature women keep their looks and their figures. They don't put on weight and turn into great big puddings like the Polynesians. And they walk well. You ever noticed how they walk? That's from carrying all those pots and bundles and stuff on their heads.'

There was a lengthy silence. He still stared at his glass. 'It would be easy to live with a native woman,' he murmured at last. 'If you can live that way, I mean. Live in one of those open-sided houses under the bare thatch, eat their food. It's a cheap way of living, you don't need many clothes in this climate, nor any heat. Only a little cooking fuel, a little money for rice and fish, and . . . and a lot of money for whisky of course.'

That reminded him to empty his glass and pour fresh drinks.

' 'Going native,' they call it,' he went on, standing with the bottle in his hand. 'That's a term of abuse, of scorn. As if there's something holy about living in a great big bungalow with ten rooms and a refrigerator for keeping the fillet steak. And a white woman who never quits griping about the heat and the help, and busts a gut trying to keep up with the Joneses.'

'Not easy to shake off the trappings of a different civilisation,' I commented, 'the ingrained habits of an accustomed life-style.'

'I'm coming near to it,' he muttered softly. 'I'm coming pretty damn near to it.' He took his chair and stared at his glass again. There was another long silence.

'There is one thing I would like to ask you,' I said eventually. 'About this man Vetran. You said before his name seemed familiar.'

'Yes, I recall. I've heard that name from somewhere. I wish I could remember.' He scratched the bristles on his chin.

'I bumped into him recently. A businessman of some sort, he has an office in town.'

'It's coming to me,' Max said slowly. 'A businessman, that's right. He owns a number of shops or at least rents out the premises. He is in a fair way of business, I believe.'

'What sort of shops does he have?'

'I have no idea. My guess would be the usual sort, the shops that sell the cloth and the batiks — there's scads of them — maybe a jeweller's.'

'Or a photographer's?'

He gave me a curious glance. 'There are two or three photographer's businesses in town,' he said carefully, 'yes, he might have one of them.'

'Well, it's not important. I was curious, that's all.' I finished my drink and moved to the door.

'Let me know what you hear, Max,' I said. 'I'm still in the market for information.'

'Sure will,' he grunted, 'and drop round again. Nice talking with you.'

I went out and across the strip of rough ground, into the passage and through the hallway to the street. The three gamblers took not the slightest notice of me. I might not have existed: I didn't figure in their world. I turned left out of the hotel and almost immediately I was swallowed up in the shadows beyond the streetlights.

18

It was another hot night. The breeze came in exhausted little flutters as if all its energy had drained away, and the grass underfoot was parched and crackled to the tread. In the distance, over the mountains, thunder muttered faintly and lightning drew jagged patterns across the sky. There was a soft drinks stand across the way, a wooden hut with a bench and half a dozen customers who sat and stood and talked and laughed. It stood opposite the Hotel Lavinia but a hundred yards further down the road, and it looked like a good place for me to wait. I knew there was some waiting to be done.

I bought a bottle of Seven-up with a straw and took it into the shadow of the corner of the hut. Standing there I had an uninterrupted view of the hotel entrance, and I wasn't so obvious as if I stood among the group of Balinese.

Time went by, quite a lot of time.

Three bottles of Seven-up, and that means a very long time indeed. I began to think it hadn't worked, he hadn't taken my bait, that what I'd said about Zahl and the connection between the two of them hadn't got him worried. Nor yet my heavy hint about Vetran and a photographer's shop. It was all guesswork anyway: I might very well be knocking on the wrong door.

I'd been there an hour and a half and I couldn't take any more of that kid's stuff. It was a no-show and I had to try something else.

Then he came out. I could see even at that distance that he had stopped to shave, change his clothes and generally clean himself up. But he was not dressed for somewhere smart: just his usual white shoes and slacks and a gay multicoloured shirt. He should not be too hard to follow.

He turned right towards the town and away from me. That suited me very well. I waited till he had gone fifty yards and then I casually started after him.

He walked steadily, not fast, but with

purpose. I was afraid he would find a solitary taxi and take off to leave me stranded. Taxis cruised by but he kept on walking. He crossed the junction at the end of the road, bore round towards the old royal palace and then right along the narrow street that led to the market. I kept behind a good hundred yards, paused in the well-lighted areas as if I were a casual stroller, and hurried to catch up across the dark places. He passed the market, now dark and deserted, and crossed the bridge beyond. I thought he might turn left into the night market on the far side of the bridge, get himself something to eat at one of the native food stalls, but he kept right on. He turned by the cinema at the corner and paused at the big road junction, as if making up his mind over something. I was too close now, dangerously close, and I stopped and studied the display cabinets outside the cinema. They had Clint Eastwood in a spaghetti Western, his eyes screwed up characteristically, face mean, that thin chewed cheroot in his mouth. In the far cabinet they had stills from the next show, some space oddysey in which the characters were surrounded by massed dials and switchboards and wore awkward-looking futuristic garb on bodies that were pretty standard 1980s models.

He'd made up his mind and crossed the road and I was held up by traffic. He'd gone down a dark street over to the right and I thought I'd lost him. I walked faster. I got a glimpse of white slacks by the corner of an alley, a good two hundred yards ahead. I took a chance and sprinted as far as the alley. He was going up there, slowly now, picking his way through the mud, the broken gutter that ran down the centre, the rotting garbage, plastic containers and discarded cans, the excrement of dogs and mules and perhaps of humans too. I could never understand how Denpasar was not a good deal smellier, nor alive with ants, cockroaches and flies and all the creatures that feed on human waste.

The alley was pretty much deserted. At the lower end there were one or two food stalls still doing business, and what looked like a native guest-house. Then it was all little shops, wooden boxes just big enough to hold a small display and room for one or two persons to get around it, now all dark and shuttered. I saw the white legs proceed carefully up about two-thirds of the alley, and then they were gone. I followed him to the same point. A narrow entrance ran off to one side into a cluster of walls and yards enclosing the kind of open-sided thatched dwellings, raised a few feet from the ground, that Max had spoken of.

I went very cautiously now, very quietly, trying not to disturb a dog or stumble over a loose step. I heard voices: low, a little distant, but one of them familiar. The voices came from a house at the end of a long narrow courtyard and its lamp illuminated the whole area to within a few feet of where I stood. I made those few feet and stopped at the very edge of the light. I couldn't distinguish any words. I could hear enough to be certain of only one thing. Max was talking to a woman.

Their conversation continued for some

little time, the voices subdued and even, nothing to suggest alarm, anger or any strong emotion. I gave it up and retreated further from the light and waited. They must have talked for a long half-hour when I heard different noises. He was coming back. He passed within a few feet of me and I let him get as far as the alley, waited a minute longer, and followed. When I reached the alley he was half-way down it, picking his way as before but rather more quickly. I went back into the courtyard and stood within the circle of light thrown by the lamp, at the foot of the three or four stone steps that led up to the house.

The room was divided by a curtain, and whoever was there was on its far side. That was why the voices had been indistinct. I climbed the few steps, drew aside the curtain and stood on the margin of the space beyond.

There were mats and baskets and a few pieces of low furniture. The lamp that had bothered me was on my side of the curtain and the room beyond was shaded from its brightness. A small, slim woman sat with her back to a wooden partition on my left. She squatted on a bundle of mats and some brightly coloured cloth that she had been sewing lay by her lap. She had glossy black hair, with the elaborate arrangement piled up on one side of the head that is favoured by tradition, smooth almond-coloured skin, brown eyes, a straight, somewhat broad nose, very red painted lips and a petite and pretty chin. She wore a flowered sarong and bodice and there were silver bangles on her arms.

For one long moment she continued to stare at the floor, and then, as if she had only just noticed the movement of the curtain, the intrusion of my shoes within her line of vision, she looked up and eyed me with a calm, unpanicked gaze.

'Good evening,' I said. 'I apologise for disturbing you.'

'Good evening,' she replied softly and smoothly, with little trace of accent, 'come in, please.'

'May I have the pleasure of knowing your name?'

'My name is Sadowa. Please sit down, Mr Ingram.'

'You know who I am.'

'I was told that a gentleman named Mr Ingram might come to see me here. I was given a very detailed description of that gentleman. The description fits you exactly and therefore I think you must be Mr Ingram. But please sit down.'

There was only the floor or a low wooden stool that was placed immediately in front of her. I chose the stool. She gazed at me with the quietest of eyes, the most open of faces.

'You have come about the pearls?'

'That is correct. Do you know where they are now, who has them?'

'Yes.'

There was a dream-like, unreal quality about the conversation.

'Would you be prepared to tell me who has the pearls?'

'I am prepared to have them brought here.'

'And you would allow me to take them away?'

'No.'

'Ah. There would be a reward, of course. A large sum of money.'

'Money is not necessary. If it pleases you to give me money for my small service it is well. I ask for none.'

'Then what do you want in exchange for the pearls?'

'I wish to see the lady.'

'The lady who owns the pearls?'

'Yes. I will give the pearls to her. Only to her.'

'So if I bring the lady here you will give her the pearls, without condition?'

'Yes.'

'How soon can this be done?'

'Within the hour.'

I felt the perspiration starting on my forehead. My shirt was clinging moistly to my body. The room was very warm and airless though the woman who sat calmly gazing at me looked as unruffled as the Mona Lisa. That was on the spur of the moment, but appropriate. There was a mysterious smile on her lips, not unlike the original, not unlike at all. But it was not the room or the hot night that had me sweating. It was the woman. Sadowa, she said. Sadowa was going to return the pearls. Within the hour and without condition. And only minutes after Max Coffman had talked with her. It didn't make sense, it didn't remotely begin to make sense.

I stood up to get at my handkerchief, wiped my brow and studied her at the same time. She was not tall, but her figure was elegant. Age, difficult to guess. Not very young. Max was right. The mature women here kept their looks and their figure.

'Within the hour,' I repeated. 'It may take me a little longer than that to bring the lady here, perhaps two or three hours.'

'That is well. She must come in person.'

'Why? Why must she come in person? Would you explain why I cannot take them?'

'I will explain it. If you will please not smile at the explanation.'

'I won't smile.'

'Then if you will sit and listen patiently I will tell you a story.'

I went back to the stool that was much too small for me. She leaned a little forward as if to emphasise her words.

'Many, many years ago these pearls were brought to Bali by a prince, a great prince of Java. He brought them in order to gain the hand of a princess of the island, a most beautiful princess. Many other princes had sought her hand in marriage. They brought rubies, emeralds and other precious stones, gold, elephants and many valuable things. But she had refused them all. Until the prince from Java brought the pearls. These were the most beautiful thing she had ever seen. She accepted the prince and on the wedding day he gave her the pearls. That very night he died, mysteriously. The pearls went afterwards to the sister of the princess and so down in the family, but to every person who owned them came great misfortune. A sudden death of a loved one, a strange incurable illness or fits of madness. The pearls were cursed.'

I used the handkerchief again, but automatically. I couldn't take my eyes off her face. There was a strange intensity now in her expression, her eyes had a hypnotic effect.

'What caused the curse?' I asked softly.

'The curse is the vengeance of Siva. Siva, our god. The pearls, you see, were so large, so beautiful, that they had been given to Siva. The prince who brought them here, who died on his wedding night, stole them from the temple of Siva, the great temple of Perembetan. The wrath of Siva has followed them ever since. No one who keeps the pearls can escape it. That is why they must be returned to the lady who has them. She is already cursed. When they are returned to her they will harm no one else, until she gives them to another person.'

'Is there no way of breaking the curse?'

'The wrath of Siva will end when the pearls are restored to the temple. Not until then. Until that time whoever keeps the pearls will suffer.'

There was a long silence. I waited to see if there was more, but now she picked up the piece of material by her side and began to sew. I got up and moved back to the curtain. 'I will come back with the lady,' I said. 'It would be better if you did not tell her of the curse. I respect your story, but I do not think she would believe it.'

'It is not important. She is already cursed.'

'Yes.'

I pulled aside the curtain, went down the steps and out through the courtyard. I stumbled down the alley and walked quickly towards the lights of the town.

19

The distant thunder rolled more menacingly and the lightning flashed incessantly as I was admitted by the pretty servant girl with the shy smile. She ushered me into the big sitting-room with the delicate flowered mats, the exotic draperies, lacquered tables and enamelled vases full of flowers. The four cane easy chairs stood in their places round the teakwood table. Three of them were occupied.

'Why, hello, Harry,' Andrée exclaimed, 'join the party and get merry like us. You're just in time to make a fourth for bridge.' Her eyes were unnaturally bright, her face a little flushed.

'How are you?' asked Carl formally. 'Yes, Andrée is right. We are a little dull tonight. Bridge is a good idea.'

'Another drink would be a better one,' said Jacky. 'What are we all having?'

I settled for Scotch and sank into the big cushions of the fourth chair. Jacky brought cards and Carl began to shuffle them.

'I'm sorry to put a damper on the bridge,' I said, 'this is a business call, and the business is urgent.'

Carl licked his lips. 'You have information about the pearls?'

'Briefly, yes. But I think it is information I ought to discuss with Andrée, in private.'

Andrée put down her glass clumsily, noisily. 'Private be damned, Harry. All of us know about the pearls. We can discuss it here.'

'The trouble is I know what I have to say, and you don't.' I glanced round at the other two. Carl and Jacky looked straight-faced. 'It would be better in private, if you don't mind.'

'But I do mind,' she cried, her voice a little high. 'Tell me now, here.'

The small man in the white sarong and crisp jacket brought in the drinks. There was uneasy silence while he went with them from chair to chair and left again. I decided I would tell only what was absolutely necessary, the bare minimum.

The three of them looked at me expectantly.

'All right, if that's the way you want it. I am in touch with someone who is in a position to return the pearls, tonight.'

'Tonight? Amazing! And just who may this someone be?' Andrée was more flushed now. The hand which held the glass was not quite steady.

'A woman, a Balinese woman, in Denpasar.'

'Why, Harry, I had no idea the dusky native beauties attracted you. But there's no accounting for taste.'

'Let's be serious,' I growled. 'We're not talking about some heap of dime-store paste. We're talking about a million dollars. Unless I've been taken for a ride the pearls are there now, just waiting to be picked up.'

'Where?' asked Jacky.

'I told you, in Denpasar. I haven't an address but I can take Andrée straight there.'

'Why not pick them up yourself?' asked Carl thoughtfully. 'Is a reward required?'

'No, no reward. Andrée can just go and

pick them up. But only Andrée. The woman won't give them to anyone else. She has reasons for that.'

'It sounds so wonderfully mysterious,' said Andrée. 'Some unnamed native woman, obscure but no doubt beautiful, in some unknown residence set in that jewel of the east, Denpasar. And at the same time wonderfully simple. I just go, come back with the pearls and it doesn't cost me a cent.'

'That's it.'

'There must be a catch,' Carl mused. 'Why should anyone return the pearls without a reward?'

'There isn't time to go into it,' I rasped. 'The fact is I've located the pearls and they can be got back at no cost.' I strode over to Andrée's chair, took the glass from her hand, put one arm under her shoulders and yanked her to her feet.

'Oh, Harry,' she mocked, 'how masterly of you. I go for the cave-man approach.'

I slapped her hard across the face. Her eyes widened enormously and one hand crept instinctively to her cheek where it stung red. 'Sober up,' I bellowed fiercely.

'Can't you understand what I'm saying? This isn't a game. The pearls are there for the asking.'

She stared at me wide-eyed, her hand to her cheek. I picked up the slim bag that was down by her chair and thrust it in the other hand. I took her firmly by the arm and walked her out of the room and through into the hall. She began to sob.

'There was no call to be rough,' she cried at last. 'I would have come eventually, when I was ready.'

'Eventually isn't good enough.'

'There was no need to slap me, humiliate me.'

'Someone ought to have done it years ago.'

I marched her out through the main door and across the crunching gravel to the Mercedes.

'Keys in your bag?'

'Yes,' sulkily.

I unclasped the bag and found the keys among the comb, the lipstick, the handkerchiefs, the other bric-à-brac. I pushed her into the passenger seat and went round and got in behind the wheel.

I fumbled the keys into the ignition.

'You're taking over my car now.'

'Don't be childish. You're not fit to drive.'

She sat staring straight ahead as I turned the car out on to the road and drove into Denpasar.

'Carl and Jacky know about Zahl?' I asked her.

'Yes.'

'You told them?'

'No.' She paused. 'They must have heard some other way.'

I drove on through the town, round by the cinema where a huge Clint Eastwood scowled from the hoarding, screwing up his eyes, surprised perhaps to find himself so far from the prairies. We crossed the big junction, went down the dark road and stopped by the alley.

'We walk from here,' I growled.

I took her arm and helped her pick her way through the debris of the alley. Her high heels made hard work of the potholes and loose stones. I guided her up the entrance to the courtyard. 'This is it. I'll do the talking. You just try and be sensible for once.'

She didn't reply. I let go her arm and we went up the steps to the house. I pulled back the curtain.

The woman was still in her place, exactly where she had been less than two hours before, and her sewing was on her lap. But her body was doubled up at the waist, the face almost touching the thighs. I gripped Andrée's arm. We both stood stock-still. Then I let her go, stepped across to the woman, grasped her shoulders and pulled her trunk upright. The eyes were still calm, unblinking, the smile serene and mysterious. A great patch of blood stained the flowered bodice, and from the upper part of the stain protruded the carved handle of a kris. Ten inches of kris had entered her and sealed that Mona Lisa smile for ever.

20

I felt an arm, a wrist. No pulse, almost cold. The killer could have been waiting for me to leave. I got Andrée back in the car and drove away from there. She was plenty sober now. I could see her hands tightly clenched, the knuckles showing white, the line of her jaw unnaturally high, taut and rigid. She hung on until we got back to the house and then came the collapse. She put her head on my shoulder and the tears flowed fast. I got her inside and rang for the maid, I held her while her whole body shook with great sobs. This was worse than the time before, when she'd seen Zahl stretched out on his cabin floor, a lot worse.

'Oh, Harry,' she sobbed, 'I killed her.'

'Don't be absurd,' I said brutally, 'you had nothing to do with it.'

'It was the pearls, don't you see, the pearls that killed her.'

The maid was there now. I told her to

take Andrée to her room by the garden way and make sure she took a sedative and went to bed. I said it all over once more and glared at the little girl very sternly. 'You understand what I have said?'

She smiled and nodded carefully, quite unperturbed. 'I understand.'

I saw them go out through the garden door, the short, slight figure of the calm Balinese supporting the distraught, taller woman. Then I went to the sitting-room. It was a very nice evening there, cheerful and amusing. Jacky and Carl were playing vingt-et-un. They looked up at me enquiringly.

'Andrée has gone to bed,' I muttered shortly, 'she is not very well. The evening has been a strain for her.'

Carl raised his eyebrows. 'She had rather a lot to drink earlier. Nothing serious, I hope?'

'No, nothing serious.'

'Perhaps Jacky or I should go to her.'

'Frankly I don't think she would welcome anyone at the moment.'

'Oh, I see.'

Jacky studied the cards in her hand. 'And the pearls?'

'There was a hitch. We couldn't get them.'

'Uh-huh. I thought it sounded much too easy.'

'Yes, it did, didn't it?'

I threw myself into a chair and looked at them. How much did they know? What did they understand that I had not begun to comprehend?

'Where do you go from here?' Carl asked.

'I have no idea.'

'I expect you could use a drink,' he said. 'You did not finish your last one. Scotch, wasn't it?'

I nodded wearily. He didn't wait to call the man-servant but left the room to fetch it himself. Jacky smiled at me over her cards.

'Get rid of him,' I said quietly, 'I've got to talk to you.'

'Again? I am enjoying the game.'

'Just get rid of him.'

Carl came back with a very large drink in his hand. 'It is all I could find, a blend called Highland Pride — you approve?'

'I wouldn't care if it were Highland Privy,' I growled coarsely. 'As long as it's seventy proof and makes this grey world bright again.' I took half of it at a swallow.

'You are disappointed, of course,' Carl murmured soothingly.

'I'm disappointed, devastated and damn near defunct. These pearls are damned elusive, as the Scarlet Pimpernel would have said.'

'The Scarlet Pimpernel?'

'Never mind. Before your time, long before your time.'

Carl had new cards in his hand. 'Are you twisting?'

Jacky pursed her lips. 'Twist.' He gave her a card from the top of the pack.

'That does it,' she smiled, 'bust.'

He made a note on a scorecard, then turned to me. 'That was strange about Herr Zahl, not so?'

'Very strange.'

'I mean that Andrée and you should have found him dead there on his boat.'

'That too.'

'Do you think his death had something

to do with the pearls?'

'Your guess is as good as mine. Perhaps better.'

He turned back to the cards and shuffled for a new game. They played happily with smiles and little jokes. I felt the whisky burn my stomach. It didn't do any good. All the time I saw Sadowa with the blood on her bodice, the cold sharp steel piercing her heart.

Carl was totting up the scorecard. 'I have nearly caught up with you,' he called cheerily, 'just a few more hands.'

'I think you had better go, Carl,' Jacky murmured sweetly.

'Go, why?'

'Well, it is after one, and Harry is very tired.'

'Harry very tired? What has that to do with it?' He looked quickly at me and back at Jacky. She had a curious smile on her lips. He coloured slightly.

'Oh, I see. Three's a crowd, of course. How stupid of me.'

He rose immediately, pecked Jacky primly on the forehead and waved at me.

'I will call for a taxi from the hall,' he

cried. 'Goodnight, Harry, I hope you will have success — with the pearls I mean.'

'Thanks. Particularly with the pearls.'

His steps echoed on the walkway outside.

'That was a little primitive,' I grunted, 'and possibly misleading.'

Her lips wore the same odd smile. She shrugged her shoulders. 'Primitive perhaps, misleading no. Do you want me here or in the bedroom?'

'That's misleading too. I just want to talk to you. I don't care where it is.'

She came over and picked up my glass. 'Empty. I have some much better Scotch in my room, the kind you specified — Glenfiddich. I ordered it specially.'

'Seems a pity not to use it.'

We went through the garden and over to her room. The Glenfiddich stood on her dressing table. I opened it and poured two large tots. We took the drinks on the verandah, as we had done the previous night. Lightning seared the whole horizon now. Some of the thunder was directly overhead, bursting with the roar of heavy artillery. Large rainspots marked the

208

concrete of the path like a sudden fever rash.

I wasn't sure whether the Glenfiddich was keeping me going or sending me to sleep. My head pounded with the pressure of the bursting storm, the recurrent image of the woman with the kris in her heart. We sat there silently while the storm rolled all around, gathering strength for its climacteric.

Jacky asked quietly: 'Where did you take Andrée tonight?'

I sighed wearily. 'To see a woman in Denpasar. I thought she would give me back the pearls.'

'How did you find her in the first place?'

'I followed Max from his hotel. He went to see her, a little earlier.'

She was silent for a long time. 'How did you know he would go there?'

'I didn't. But I'd talked to him before that. I said some things that might have worried him. And that was where he led me.'

I was so tired I hardly knew what I was saying. Only that certain things had still to be said. My head spun. I seemed to be in a vast black tunnel, an endless void with only the lightning and the thunder and the constant vision of that bloodstain and kris.

'What was it you said to Max?'

'I just gave him to understand that I knew a little more about him than he imagined.'

She laughed bitterly. 'We're like two complete strangers, sitting side by side in a plane, or meeting by chance in a bar. Neither knows what the other guy may know or think, and so neither wants to say too much in case it gives something vital away.'

She swallowed Scotch, leaned back in her chair, and looked at me speculatively: 'I wonder if I under-rated you.'

21

'I wonder, too. Let's find out.'

I fetched the bottle and freshened up the drinks. 'I'll tell it as I've worked it out. It won't be right in every detail, but most of the details won't matter.'

I swallowed Scotch and tried to concentrate. I had to forget what had happened that night.

'You met Max on the West Coast, perhaps five or six years ago. At that time he was doing all right. He had his own security business. Possibly you worked for him then — it doesn't really matter. Then the business failed. Max had to take whatever job he could find. You did all right yourself: became companion to a young girl whose wealthy parents were away a lot of the time, a girl who was a little wild and needed an older woman to take care of her. How is it so far?'

'Like you said, fudgy on some of the detail.'

'OK. Then Andrée's parents were killed in the air crash and she really lost control. She began to get into liquor, drugs, doubtful company and worse places. Not long after this Max got a job in just the sort of club that Andrée frequented, the Amneris Club, which happened to be owned by a Mr Zahl. Now that is one of the only two real coincidences in the whole story, but it was crucial to what followed.'

I paused and drank Scotch. The rain spatters were coming more frequently now. 'You and Max got a little idea. It was a perfect set-up. You had the inside knowledge about Andrée and her habits, her money, and Max had the opportunity, working in the club. There was one thing you could count on. Sooner or later it would happen. She would go over the top, and when she did Max would be there with his little camera. After that it was only a matter of waiting for the right time to cash in.'

I drank more corpse-reviver. 'When she reformed, if she ever did, and you came out here, it looked nearly right. Andrée started to go steady with Carl, she might decide to marry him. And Carl is ambitious. He wants to get places. He would be the last man to want those photographs splashed on the front page of some scandal sheet. It might not worry Andrée too much, but him — definitely. The time was not really quite right for you because she wasn't yet twenty-five and couldn't touch her capital. But it might not be wise to wait because she and Carl might so easily break up, and she did have the pearls. How is it now?'

'Inspired,' she breathed softly. 'Mister, you should be writing scripts for television. You're wasted here.'

'Let's take it a bit further. Carl comes into the picture now. He wants to buy the photographs but he needs dough. So he lets drop a story about finding gold in Sumatra. Nobody wants to take that bait. The only solution is to sell the pearls. Carl offers to handle the whole thing, sell the pearls and get back the photographs, and Andrée agrees to a little plan to cover up the pearls' disappearance. It has to look as if they were stolen, not in order to claim on the insurance — no company would have paid in any case — but simply to explain why she wasn't wearing them any more. But who is going to buy them? Now here we come to the second coincidence, and the one that makes it really interesting. Carl happens to know Zahl — they've both been knocking around the islands for some time — and Zahl was the kind of man who had the money and the interest in this kind of local antique to offer a deal.'

A great blast of lightning and an instantaneous cannonade brought down the storm. Rain hammered on the paths and blew into the verandah. We fled into the room and shut the windows against the rain. The Scotch had me going now and I wasn't about to let a little tropical storm stop me. She could have stripped naked and shown me a couple of tickets for the next flight to Tahiti and I'd have still kept going. There were neither tickets nor temptation. All she did in fact was top up the drinks once more and sit herself demurely on a chair, the knowing smile still on her lips.

'You just got to Zahl,' she smiled sweetly. 'Who bumped him off and why?'

'Let's not jump the gun — in more senses than one. When Carl took the pearls to Zahl he took them to the one person who could connect the pearls with the photographs. It may have been set up that way: Zahl as the middleman, so that Max's cover, and yours, wouldn't be blown. Neither of you could come out into the open. Or Zahl may have known about the photographs all along and just put two and two together. Either way he held the key. He could play the game according to his own rules. He got the pearls and he had to have the photographs, too. He offered to deal direct with the blackmailer and Carl was only too happy to let him do it.'

Her smile was a little scornful now. 'All guesswork. You have no real idea how much Zahl knew, what he did.'

'It's the way it fits. Someone — the blackmailer — passed the photographs to Zahl, but before that he had new negatives and prints made — the originals of the ones that were shown to me.'

'Then this someone rubbed Zahl — to get the pearls. Who?'

'Well, who could it be? I can't see it could be you, and I know it wasn't Andrée. And Carl had no motive. He doesn't know of the extra photographs, and still doesn't, I imagine. That leaves Max. He saw the game slipping from his fingers. Zahl had double-crossed him. Max hadn't got the pearls and he hadn't got the dough. It would be time for a showdown.'

She sat staring at her glass, thinking, calculating. 'What do you do now?' she asked without expression. 'Tell the police? Get him arrested?'

'No, not for a little while. I'm prepared to offer a deal.'

'A deal?'

'Yes. You are finished here, and so is Max. Max returns the pearls and I'll talk to Andrée about a golden farewell.'

'You're serious about this?'

'Perfectly.'

'I suppose there's no other way out.'

'No.'

She finished her drink and pressed her

lips together reflectively. 'I'll talk to Max. Give me a little time.'

'Only a very little. Twelve hours, no more. There's nothing to consider. If you run with the loot you have the problem of disposal. The pearls are hot, too hot to sell. And broken up they wouldn't fetch much. That's why Zahl showed them to me: he thought I might get him an offer from the insurance company. And if Max has another set of photographs he's no longer in a sellers' market. Someone else has them, too — they're not exclusive property any more. And I don't think Andrée is interested. It was Carl who got all hot and bothered, and he has no money.'

'You have it all worked out, except for one thing. Maybe Max doesn't have the pearls or the photographs.'

'If not, he knows where they are.'

She went over to the dressing table and stared at her face in the mirror. 'Seems a pity it had to end this way,' she said slowly, 'we never made it together.'

I stood behind her and stared at the two reflections. Hers was smooth, fresh, deceivingly innocent; mine tired, strained, wrinkled round the eyes.

'It wasn't to be,' I murmured. 'With Andrée it's a game, for kicks, nothing else. You told me so and she told me so. With you it was another kind of game. Meant to distract me, blind me, milk me of what I knew or had guessed. Like leading me to Max and pushing Carl as the villain. Clever women can be so stupid. They think men can never see through their little games or resist their irresistible bodies.'

'It's not too late to see how irresistible mine can be.'

'It's much too late.'

I was filled with sudden, overwhelming revulsion. There had been too much deceit. Too much sex had been thrown at me. And too much evil, pain and death. I touched her lightly on the cheek with one finger and got out of there.

22

The storm had moved away to the south when the taxi dropped me at the hotel. Lightning flashes were still visible in the distance, beyond the airport and out over the sea, the rumble of thunder faint and fading. The desk was closed and locked up but on the wall was pinned an envelope that had my name on it. The envelope contained my room key and a message from the desk clerk: 'Sir, a lady called while you were out. She asks that you will be so kind as to meet her at the royal temple of Mengwi as soon as possible. Message left at 11.30 p.m.'

Eleven-thirty. That was about the time Andrée and I had left to find the pearls and found instead a corpse. I looked at my watch: five thirty-five a.m. I thought of cool water cascading from the shower, clean, fresh sheets, blessed oblivion that my brain and body cried out for. I went out to the stretch of grass in front of the hotel and breathed in the rain-cooled air. The air and the puddles were the only reminders of the storm.

The same taxi stood silently down by the road, the driver counting his takings, deciding whether to call it a night. He looked up at me in surprise.

'Take me to Mengwi?'

'Now? Mengwi? The temple?'

'Yes, and wait to bring me back — perhaps an hour. Can do?'

He paused and thought. 'Can do.'

Streaks of light were in the eastern sky when we skirted the lake and stopped by the entrance to the temple. The vague outlines of the cluster of little buildings could just be made out. I left the taxi on the road and followed the pathway. Mengwi, on the road to Singaradja. Did that mean anything?

With each step, almost, the light grew, the rapid rise of a tropical dawn.

I climbed the steps to the upper level and began to walk slowly down the long avenue between the buildings. A slim, small figure emerged from the darkness of the last of the pavilions, a figure with a long flowered skirt and bodice and a covering of the same material over the head. I got to within five paces of her before I was quite sure it was Zahl's wife, his widow.

She wore plain leather sandals on her feet now, not golden ones, but otherwise she was just the same, the face enigmatic, the eyes unblinking, the lips firm. She showed no sign of strain or fatigue. And there was something in her features that I hadn't noticed before, something that was vaguely familiar, but would not come to mind.

'You have waited all night in the storm,' I said. 'I came as soon as I received your message.'

'I sheltered here and was safe. I knew you would come.'

She moved into the darkness of the pavilion. On the stone step sat a large bag made of raffia with carved wooden handles. They reminded me of another carved handle I had seen lately. She stooped and took from the bag a slender box and handed it to me. I turned the simple metal catch and opened it. There was a sealed envelope and under that lay the dull gold, the dark rubies, the milky sheen of the pearls.

I closed the box and held it in one hand. 'You wish me to return these?'

'Yes. They cannot do her more harm. She is already cursed.'

'Another woman told me the same thing last night, before she died.'

She nodded and her lips trembled for one moment. 'She was my sister.'

She turned away as if to indicate the meeting was over. I put my free hand on her arm and she stood motionless.

'Why did you kill her?'

My voice held no strain, no tension, only tiredness. I might have been asking about the swatting of a fly.

She half turned and faced me again. There was no fear in her face, no emotion in her eyes. They were dead eyes.

'Because she was about to commit a great sin.' She paused, as if the effort of finding the right words was a huge burden. 'She was going to live with the man who killed my husband, the white man, Max. They were going away last night, far from Bali, where the wickedness would not be known.'

I released her arm. 'She was going to give back the pearls.'

'Yes. She could not keep them, and she would not let the man keep them — or the photographs. She did not wish the curse to fall on her as it has fallen on my husband.'

'So you brought the pearls to me. Why did you ask me to come here?'

She glanced around her. The rising sun was turning the sandy ground to gold, restoring afresh the sleeping colours of the shrines. 'It is a holy and beautiful place. Siva is here, and Siva will understand what I have had to do. I killed with the blessing of Siva, with a holy kris. Now I must go.' She picked up her bag and turned away again.

'One last question: Were you there when your husband was murdered?'

She stopped, kept her face turned away from me. 'Yes, I was there on the boat. But not below, I sleep up in the bows on the deck when I wish to be alone. I heard the shot, I saw the man go and I recognised him. He had been to the boat before, and I knew he was the one who loved my sister.'

'Goodbye,' I said softly, 'and thank you for these.'

She nodded. There was another long pause while she decided what she would say. 'I have two holy kris,' she murmured at last.

'Yes.'

I walked quickly down the avenue of shrines. At the top of the steps I stopped and looked back. The sun lighted up the whole temple now. Only the interiors of the pavilions were still shaded from the light. I could just make out a shape in the shadow of the last building. I went down the steps to the waiting car.

23

It was noon and I was back in the Vetran hothouse. The overgrown grounds were green and shining after the rain and the sun drew up the moisture in a cloud of steam. I was drinking Pouilly fuissé and sweating a little in reaction to the chill of the wine. The atmosphere in the room was close and sticky — no worse than a Singapore street on one of its stickier days, but who wants to be out in a Singapore street?

Vetran stood smiling at me, the elegant wine glass in his hand. 'Well, Mr Ingram, have you come to take up my offer?'

'No. I checked back, as I said I would. You haven't anything to sell. The lady really isn't interested in your merchandise. Also, I got to the intermediary myself.'

'You shoot a good line in bluff, Mr Ingram.'

'If you think I'm bluffing you were

never so mistaken in your life.'

'Nevertheless, I do not hesitate to call it. Can you substantiate what you say?'

I had my handkerchief out and was wiping off my forehead and neck. 'You should get air-conditioning' I bellowed, 'this Turkish bath is losing you business.'

'Please do not prevaricate, Mr Ingram.'

'I'm not prevaricating. I'm sweating, and not because I'm trying to bamboozle you.' I put away the damp rag that was my handkerchief. 'So far as the photographs go, you admit yours are only copies and someone else held the originals. That weakens your hand. You assume the someone else is putting on the pressure, but that's only an assumption and you don't know whether it's working. If the originals won't work then yours won't either. As for the name you could sell me, I'm ahead of you. It's a woman called Sadowa and I think I know how you got on to her.'

I put the handkerchief to work again. He poured more wine and still smiled.

'You have some businesses in town,' I

went on. 'One of them is a photographer's shop. A while ago a Balinese woman brought in some negatives for prints to be made. The man in the shop recognised the subject of the negatives. He told you about them and you thought you'd just picked up the spare key to Fort Knox. Then when the woman came back to collect you had her followed and found out who she was. You guessed, of course, that she was acting to cover the real owner of the pictures.'

'Very ingenious.'

'The possibilities were not very great. I couldn't imagine any other way that you could have come to have the photographs. Now, I think you are going to give me what you have and call it a day.'

'I am? Why?'

'Because last night the woman Sadowa was murdered.'

That dented his smile a trifle. I was about to dent it a lot more.

'You can check into it if you don't believe me, but it would be a whole lot smarter to keep clear. Her death is connected with the photographs, you need have no doubt of that. And when the police begin to poke around and get to hear that you were trying to peddle the same photographs they are liable to put two and two together and make it come out as Vetran.'

He stood and thought, drank a little more wine. 'And if I give you the photographs you will keep my name out of it?'

'Neither of us is a gentleman, but we could agree on it.'

He moved quickly into the next room and I heard the same sounds I'd heard that other time. He returned with the envelope and passed it to me.

I checked quickly through the contents.

'It seemed a good idea,' he smiled ruefully, 'fool-proof almost.'

'You need luck too,' I smiled back, 'and all your luck got used up in the first break, when the photographs came into your shop. There just wasn't any more left over.'

I went out to the waiting taxi. The driver had curled up on the back seat as if he'd expected a long wait. Perhaps he'd been to the Vetran place before.

Now I was there with the fat stone figures. I grinned back at them. I could afford to. I was there for the last time.

I padded after the shy girl in the batik into the big sitting-room. Andrée was there looking much too small for one of the great cane chairs, a cigarette smouldering from long tapering fingers and cerise nails.

'Oh, Harry, I'm so glad to see you.'

'You're feeling better?'

'Oh, yes. But more terrible things have happened. Jacky has gone. She just packed up and left.'

'I had an idea she might.'

'And, what do you think? She went down to that awful hotel where Max stayed.'

'The Lavinia?'

'Yes. And when she got there the police were swarming all over.'

'Max had been murdered.'

She stared at me, unbelieving. 'How did you know?'

'I had a hint, very early this morning, from a lady at the temple of Mengwi.'

'Mengwi? Temple? What on earth are you talking about?'

'It's too complicated to explain. Go on with your story.'

'Jacky rang me from the police headquarters. It's all very strange. Max was killed by a kris — just the same as — '

'As last night.'

'Yes. And the police are holding Jacky.'

'They'll let her go. The police can't prove anything, and in Jacky's case there is nothing to prove. She wasn't involved in the murder.'

'She doesn't want to come back.'

'That's very simple. It was she and Max who were putting the bite on you over the photographs. I knew it, and she has a good idea that by now you know it.'

She stared at me and murmured slowly, 'I had a feeling about it. It was staring me in the face and I just didn't want to know.' She sighed, stubbed out the cigarette. 'With Jacky gone it seems as if a whole phase, a whole chapter, of my life has come to an end.'

'It has. Forget her, forget the woman

last night, forget LA, the photographs and all that. Start again, start afresh.'

She stood up, pushing a stray wisp of hair back into place. 'Let's drink to that, Harry.'

'Yes,' I said softly, 'let's drink to that.'

We drank and we smoked and just sat quietly. I got two envelopes from my pocket and passed them to her. She glanced quickly at the photographs, coloured slightly.

'The other set, too,' I said. 'I got them back, just for the asking.'

'Harry, you're marvellous. I don't know what to say.'

She put the envelopes on the teakwood table.

'Don't leave them there,' I growled, 'lock them up, or better, burn them.'

'I think I'll put them in my photo album — to remind me of a time of my life that's gone now for ever.'

'Carl wouldn't like your keeping them.'

'I've come to the conclusion I don't much care what Carl likes.'

'I see.'

There was a faraway look in her eyes. 'I

suppose you will be going soon, leaving Bali?' she asked wistfully.

'Yes,' I said in a matter-of-fact way. 'The job is over. I have the pearls here.' I unlocked the small attaché case I'd borrowed from the hotel, took out the slender box and opened it. She looked at the pearls and then back up at me. I smiled at her. 'Now let's go and lock them away.'

We went through to the bedroom and she opened the safe. I put in the pearls and the envelopes containing the photographs. I shut the door and twirled the wheel.

'And get this combination changed.'

'Yes, sir. Any other orders?'

'Keep yourself out of trouble. I can't keep coming back to Bali to sort you out.'

'That might tempt me to be wicked again.'

She held up her face to be kissed and I kissed her. I held her slim body close to me. 'I've been trying to make up my mind about telling you something,' I whispered. 'There's pros and cons, as there always are. On balance, I think it better you should know.'

'Know what? Tell me, for heaven's sake.'

'A story attached to the pearls. A native myth — you will probably laugh at it.'

'Tell me.'

'All right. Just the essentials. In the beginning the pearls were stolen from a temple in Java, a temple of Siva. The wrath of the god pursues every one who owns the pearls. A curse, a curse that strikes the owner or persons close to the owner.'

She broke away from me and stood in the shadow of the verandah. She stared out at the massed bougainvillaea and hibiscus, the frangipani, the waving palms in the distance. 'I'm not laughing,' she cried. 'I guessed it long ago. I've always known it, without knowing why. Don't you see? My parents, and now Zahl, and Max, and the woman in Denpasar.'

I stood beside her and touched her hand. She stared in the distance still.

'Perhaps it's all over now,' she said more quietly, 'the curse has worked itself out. Siva's vengeance is complete.'

I kissed her gently on the forehead. 'I'm

certain it is,' I said.

I walked quickly through the garden to the road and my waiting taxi. I drove back to the hotel, packed, paid my bill and took another car to the airport. The Garuda flight to Jakarta and Singapore was not very full. A few Indonesian families, some western tourists, a sprinkling of businessmen. The engines roared and soon there was only the blue sea below. There was more sea and then very quickly the mountains of Java. Bali was not even a distant speck on the distant horizon.

THE END